LOVE ON REPLAY

A Berotte Family Book

MONICA WALTERS

Copyright © 2022 by Monica Walters

All rights reserved.

No part of this book may be reproduced in any form or by any electronic or mechanical means, including information storage and retrieval systems, without written permission from the author, except for the use of brief quotations in a book review.

PREFACE

Hello, readers!

Thank you for purchasing and/or downloading this book. This work of art contains explicit language, a lewd sex scene, and topics that may be sensitive to some readers. For a full disclosure, click the link below.

https://bit.ly/3N6vpO8

This book is the beginning of a new family of books... The Berotte Family (pronounced Bee-Rot). It starts with the father, and the following books will trickle down to the kids. So if some things seem incomplete where the sub characters are involved, that was done intentionally. Those issues will be resolved in their books. His daughter's, Alexz, book is next.

Also, please remember that your reality isn't everyone's reality. What may seem unrealistic to you could be very real for someone else. But also keep in mind that despite the previous statement, this is a fictional story.

PREFACE

Anissa and Sheldon have an absolutely beautiful whirlwind romance. I hope you enjoy the journey this story is going to take you on.

Monica

Dedication...

Thank you so much, Anissa Jones, for allowing me to use your name in the story and your image while promoting this work. We've known one another for a long time, and you've been supporting me on my journey as an author for a long time as well. You've done well as a single mother, and your support for Beaumont United High School is unmatched by any other. LOL!
You're a beautiful person inside and out. Continue to be the woman you are, and the woman God called you to be. Your strength while raising your two sons is admirable, and I'm pretty sure you are inspiring others, even now as they watch you handle trials and tribulations gracefully and with love.
Thanks again, and I hope you enjoy this story.

PROLOGUE

Anissa

"Anissaaaaaa! Come open the door, baby! I need you!"

I was sitting at my kitchen table, trying to eat a late dinner. I didn't leave work until late... almost two hours later than usual. The post office was working the dog shit out of my ass, and I was just about ready to retire. I had one more year, and I would be done with this shit. I dropped my spoon in my bowl of gumbo and went to the door.

"Dexter, please leave!"

It was the same shit. At least once a week, my ex-husband showed up on my doorstep, begging me to open the door. We were married for nearly twenty years when I divorced him. We had a good life together, and I just knew we would grow old together. However, when his mother died, something in him died right along with her. It started out as him popping pills to cope or smoking a blunt. It didn't take long for that to stop working though.

Within two years of her death, he'd become a full-fledged crackhead. I'd done everything I knew to do, to try to help him, but the fights and arguments were affecting our sons. Dexter Junior was sixteen, and Jamel was only twelve. Their father fighting me and practically selling everything we had took a toll on all of us. I finally made the decision to put him out. I had to look out for my kids. The police had to come here and physically remove him from the premises.

I'd changed the locks and filed a restraining order on him. Over the past fourteen years, I'd had him arrested more times than I could count. He'd gotten clean, only to relapse again. It was so damn exhausting. Now here he was, at eight o'clock, banging on my door, probably fresh off a binge. He'd been back on the streets for the past couple of years and had made my life a living hell. Truth be told, every day without the man I fell in love with was hell.

"Nissa, please, baby. I just need some help. I'm gon' get myself cleaned up, and I'm gon' do right by you."

"Dex, please don't make me call the police. I don't want to see you go to jail. Just go."

"Well, fuck you! You 'posed to love me, but whenever I need you, you always wanna call the fucking police! That's all you ever do. After all I did for you? I gave you everything I had, and you turned your back on me! Bitch!"

When the glass broke out of the window on the other side of the room, the alarm went off. He started banging on my door again, begging me to turn it off. When he saw I wasn't budging to disable it, he ran. As my cell phone rang, I went to it. I knew it was probably the police. "Hello?"

"Hello, ma'am. Do you need a unit to come out?"

They were probably tired of seeing my address. Dexter was always doing stupid shit to trip the alarm. "He left. So no. Thank you."

"Are you sure?"

"I'm sure. I'm going to call my son."

DJ would probably be here in a little bit anyway. Whenever the alarm went off, he was notified as well. "Okay. We'll send a unit by to check the premises anyway."

"Thank you."

I ended the call as I checked out the damage to my window. Sliding my hand down my face, I huffed loudly. That would have to be boarded up tonight, but I didn't want to open the door and risk Dexter showing back up. I had a gun for protection, but he was the last person I wanted to use it on. Despite everything, I still cared about him. I wanted him to get clean. Counseling nor rehab seemed to help him, and I could only attribute it to his desire to do better. It wasn't there. He didn't want to do better, and until he did, we would be fighting a losing battle trying to force him to.

I walked to my couch, flopped down on it for a moment, and lowered my face to my hands, allowing the tears to escape. After fourteen years, I still hadn't healed from the heartbreak because of shit like this. He was constantly in and out of my life. I was allowing it because I wanted him to get better. I hated him at the same time though. While I knew he was hurting from the loss of the only parent he knew, he allowed it to overtake him and make him forget about his responsibilities as a husband and father.

I made decent money at the post office, but my checks had only been used for a couple of bills. Half of it used to go to our savings account. He cleaned that out though. Thankfully, I was wise enough to have another account he couldn't touch. He didn't even know about it. If I hadn't, my boys and I would have had an even tougher time than we did. *Why did you do this to us, Dexter?* That was a recurring question I asked every time he showed up.

We were so good for one another at first... so in love. We had our issues as many married couples did, but we were always able to talk things through and come out better than we were. He was my confidant, my best friend, and my lover. He was the best father, always involved in whatever the boys were doing. We had the perfect family, the one where people looked up to us and hash tagged us as relationship goals.

The days of me laying against him while he played in my hair were long gone. The man I'd dedicated my life to no longer existed. Depression and sorrow had taken over and completely ravaged the man he once was. After a couple of years of trying to help him through it, I knew I couldn't subject my boys to his toxicity anymore. They'd already seen enough.

When I heard the door opening, I turned to see DJ walking in with a frown on his face. "I'm sick of this shit, Ma. Something needs to be done about his ass. You holding on to a man that is sick as fuck. If you don't fully let go, he gon' drag you down with him. I'm gonna go get a sheet of plywood from the garage and cover this window until I can get it fixed tomorrow. Go pack a bag. You coming to stay with me tonight."

He walked right past me, like he was the father scolding his child. DJ had always been my protector. There were plenty of fights between his father and me that he stepped in the middle of. Now that he was thirty years old, I hated he was constantly looking after me. He should have been living his own life, creating his own family. Jamel had moved to Houston last year, but before he left, he was the same way.

I didn't want to be that mother... the one who held on to her sons like they were spouses. DJ was right. I closed my eyes as the painful realization of what I was doing to myself set in. Mentally and emotionally, I was tired, stressed, and practically depleted. If I wasn't careful, that would spill over into the physical. The last thing I needed was to get sick.

Wiping my face, I took deep breaths and mouthed the words from SZA's song. *And if you wondered if I hate you, fuck you!* I needed to completely move on with my life. Loving him, hoping he would one day realize he needed to be better, was slowly killing me. I was too young to suffer that fate. Fifty-two-year-olds these days were living life to the fullest, like they were in their prime, and here I was, looking like an old maid.

Standing from my seat, I decided to put myself first from here on out. Going to my room, I packed a bag to go stay with DJ and made the decision to start fresh tomorrow by calling a realtor. I could only start fresh by disappearing from his radar altogether. It would be a hard journey, but I was up for the challenge of discovering a better me.

I

Anissa
A year and a half later...

"Great class today, ladies! Until next time."

My instructor left the class with her towel around her neck like we weren't all struggling to breathe after that intense workout. I'd been in this hip hop aerobics class for the past year and a couple of months, and this was the hardest session we'd ever had. It probably didn't help I skipped the last class to go to dinner with my boys.

Life had gotten better for me. The first few months were hard as hell. I moved to an apartment where I wouldn't have to be bothered with maintenance, taxes, and just the necessary upkeep of owning a home. I sold the house that Dexter and I had purchased during our second year of marriage, and that alone had me depressed for a couple of weeks. When DJ recommended this class, I reluctantly came, and I'd been attending ever since.

The hardest part of this transition was not knowing how Dexter was doing. At least when he popped up acting an entire fool, I at least knew he was still alive. Now, I didn't have a clue. He didn't know where I lived, and the peace I now lived in was what made me accept that I'd made the right decision.

As I rubbed my towel over my face, my friend Yolanda asked, "What are you doing when you leave? You wanna go out for drinks?"

"No. I'm tired as hell. I'm going home and relax in a hot bath and drink a glass of wine."

"That sounds good too. Well, sometime this weekend, we need to go out and celebrate your retirement. That's an accomplishment that I can't wait to get to. I'm sick of looking at that office, girl."

"Yeah, we'll see."

I grabbed my bag and promised to call her then headed to my car. I'd retired from the post office almost a month ago, and the only ones I'd celebrated with were my boys. They were both still single, playing the field, looking for their one. I knew that DJ was ready to settle down, but I wasn't so sure about Jamel. He was twenty-seven now and still having the time of his life in Houston. He came to town every other weekend to check on me, and I appreciated that.

Retirement had been everything I thought it would be. Being able to stay in bed as long as I wanted to was everything I imagined it would be as well. I'd fallen into a routine that I loved. I came to my hip hop class three days a week. Saturday mornings were usually the most fun, because more young people were here, and they got us older folks pumped up to really get into the music. I did water aerobics twice a week and lifted weights at the gym on those same days.

Sundays were my days to go to church and rest. Usually, DJ and I spent Sundays together. I saw him almost every day, but it was mainly him dropping in to check on me before he headed home. I cooked almost every day, trying out new recipes I saw on social media, and most of them were worth every minute I invested into cooking it. I was completely happy with who I had evolved into without the stress, worry, and anger.

Every morning, I meditated for at least thirty minutes. Things I found taxing before now gave me peace. Cleaning my apartment, washing clothes, and cooking nurtured the peace in my soul. As I headed home, my cell phone rang. It was only ten in the morning, so I had plans to take a wonderful nap after I soaked and had a light lunch. Seeing it was DJ, I answered. "Hey, DJ."

"What's up, Ma? What'chu doing?"

"I just left class. I'm heading home to do absolutely nothing."

"Good. I want you to go somewhere with me around three."

"Where?"

DJ liked to shop at times. It was like he would get a hair up his ass and wanted to buy out the mall. That was where most of my wardrobe came from. He was keeping me young. We were more of friends than mother and son. "A barbeque at my friend's."

"Why would I want to hang with y'all kids?"

"There will be people your age there. Jennings's parents will be there, and Chad's dad will be there also. It's at Chad's dad's house anyway. Everybody wanted to invite their peeps to come. Don't leave me hanging. They think you don't exist. I talk about you all the time, but none of them have ever seen you."

"That's 'cause I know my place. Being around you and your friends isn't something that appeals to me. I would much rather be by myself. Thank you very much. But..."

"I knew you wouldn't let me down!"

"What? I didn't say I was going," I said to mess with him.

"That was what that 'but' was for. You can't fool me, Ma. If anybody knows you, I do. See you around two forty-five."

I slightly rolled my eyes and chuckled. "Okay."

He ended the call, and I made a slight detour to Subway to get a salad. Once I got home, I ate my lunch then ran a hot bath. Typically, I wasn't around a lot of people unless I was at church or at exercise classes. DJ called me a homebody, but it wasn't that. I just enjoyed spending time with myself. I was an intelligent woman who now valued her peace. The fewer people I was around, the less I had to worry about someone disrupting my tranquility.

I spent time with Yolanda sometimes, and we only met at restaurants or the movie theater. Intentionally closing myself off to people didn't mean I wasn't friendly. I spoke and talked to people when I was out and about, but as far as letting them in to where they could actually get to know me, that was a no-go. I couldn't help but wonder if DJ was trying to get me to have more friends so he wouldn't have to check on me as much. I'd repeatedly told him I was just fine with being alone.

I stood still as I thought about that and caught a glimpse of myself in the mirror. My body was looking great, my light brown skin was glowing, and my hair was long and silky, hanging almost to my butt. People often thought that my mingled gray hair was a wig. I didn't waste my time correcting them unless they asked where I'd gotten it from. Then I'd tell them, *from my parents*. My mother had long hair, and my dad had curly hair.

Admiring my reflection had become second nature for me now. It was part of my self-love routine. *Anissa, you are beautiful, made in God's image and a reflection of His love. Keep shining, loving yourself, and being a witness of His love, and all will fall into place.* That was what kept me sane, especially in those few months after my move.

Lowering my body into the hot water that I'd sprinkled Epsom salt in, I released a sigh and a slight moan. It sounded so sexual, and every time I moaned that way, it reminded me of just how long it had been since I'd entertained a man... years. The only man that had access to my love for the past thirty-five years was Dexter Dent. He was the only man I'd ever been with. When he'd gotten clean and had stayed that way for a year or so, I'd ended up having sex with him. That was nearly four years ago.

Before that, it had been at least five years. Dexter was the only man I'd wanted... the only one I'd desired. My love for him ran deep, and it took me damn near detoxing myself of him to move on with my life. Romantically though, I was only in love with myself. I didn't go anywhere to meet anyone. When I did go places, it was like I had blinders on. I'd gotten propositioned plenty of times, but I wasn't attracted to any of them.

My spirit of discernment was at an all-time high, and it was sensitive to bullshit. I could tell within minutes what type of time a man was on. While my body craved intimacy, I knew if I never had another man to provide that, I would be okay.

I soaked in the tub for nearly an hour, then I got out. It felt like I was on the verge of falling asleep. Checking the time and seeing it was almost one o'clock, I knew I had time for an hour nap. After drying off and moisturizing my skin, I grabbed my hair wrap, then wrapped myself in my blanket, burrito style, and went straight to sleep.

2

Sheldon

"Chad, how many people did you invite? Isaiah has three coming, Shyrón has six, Dylan has two, and Alex said she has seven. That's way more people than I expected."

"Just two. Dexter and his mom," he said. "Chill out. It's gon' be cool."

"Go to the store for me and get another family pack of sausage."

I slapped a twenty in his hand then continued seasoning meat. When I told them they could invite friends, I thought they would keep it at a minimum like Chad and Dylan had done. Alexz was trying to break the damn bank with her spoiled ass. That shit was my fault though. Out of my five kids, she was the only girl and the youngest. I'd raised her alone from birth. Dylan was only a year old, and Shyrón was four when she was born, so none of them remembered their mother.

Marie had died during childbirth, and that catapulted me into single parenthood with five kids under the age of ten. My oldest, Isaiah, was nine, and Chad was seven. They remembered their mother. It was hard as hell trying to navigate through life without her, but being so busy with the kids made it a little easier.

When she passed away, I ended up quitting my job to be a full-time father, living off the couple of insurance policies she'd taken out on herself. She was an only child, so the only help I had from her side of the family was her parents, until they left this world to join her.

Having four kings and a newborn queen was extremely hard to maintain, especially because Marie had been the one that spent the most time with them. I was a lineman for Entergy and was at work a lot. So when she left, I really had to work on establishing a bond with Shyrón and Dylan. They were young and still somewhat attached to her.

Her sudden demise changed me forever. That blood clot that went to her heart had killed her nearly instantly, and there wasn't a thing anyone could have done to stop it. It happened so quickly. I became a little colder and more withdrawn. Losing love so suddenly was hard for me to digest. I was blessed with a beautiful baby girl as the love of my life took her last breath. Seeing her code and being shoved out of the room was something I would never forget.

I couldn't even grieve properly being that I had responsibilities as the man of the house. I had five kids that were looking to me for comfort. Isaiah and Chad, although they were older, still didn't understand having to go on without their mother. I didn't understand the shit, and I was thirty years old at the time. Nearly twenty-five years had flown by, and I found that I still hadn't met a woman that could even keep my attention long enough to be considered relationship material.

After seasoning the meat, I stacked the pans on top of each other and brought them outside to my pit. People would be getting here within the next hour, and I was running late with getting started. Thankfully, I'd cleaned the pit yesterday and got my fire started a little earlier. I put the steaks and pork chops on first, since they would take the longest. The chicken, sausage, and boudin would be the last to go on.

This wasn't normally my thing. Since the kids had been grown, I'd been volunteering at the high school, because some of these kids were out of control. Since I had a naturally chiseled physique, it wasn't hard to keep it that way. My stature somewhat intimidated them, and I used that to my advantage. Being that I wasn't really all that friendly, they either respected me or stayed away from me with the bullshit.

My level of patience wasn't that great either. The school was probably the last place I needed to be, but someone had to get a handle on these behavior issues they were having. My youngest was almost twenty-five, but I cared about where the future was headed. I felt like if I could step out of my comfort zone, then more people surely could, especially men.

After starting some music, I watched Isaiah and Dylan set up some tables under the tent I'd taken out of the storage shed. A lot of their friends' parents were single like me, whether they were widowed, divorced, or never married, and the boys thought it would be a good idea to get them out and get me out of my cocoon. They'd been trying to hook me up with women, but that shit wasn't working out, and I let them know I wasn't interested in them hooking me up.

When Marie died, I felt like a piece of me had died with her. I used everything I had left to raise my children to be successful, respectable adults. Now I felt like I was just a shell of a man. When school was out, I often found myself at home sleeping or doing something outside in my backyard. I'd completely redone the fence, built a deck, and did some landscaping. I tried to stay busy, because I knew I could possibly sink into a deep depression if I didn't.

I didn't really grieve Marie until my kids were much older. Because I'd waited so long to do so, the process was even longer. None of my kids were married or had families, so they stayed checking on me. Although all of them, except Alexz, had left town for school, they'd come right back. Putting them all through college and seeing them graduate was a reward like no other. I knew Marie would be so proud.

After checking the meat and seeing that the pork chops and steaks were done, I took them off the pit and loaded it with chicken. In about fifteen minutes, people would start getting here. The steak had cooked faster than normal because of all the prepping I'd done last night. Wrapping them in foil to seal in the juices had them tender as hell, and I couldn't wait to taste them.

By the time Chad had gotten back, I was putting the sausage on. He'd washed the sausage he bought and brought it to me to put on the pit along with the boudin. When he brought it to me, I noticed his friend Dexter walking up with a woman who damn near took my breath away. That shit made me nervous. In the twenty-four years Marie had been gone, that had never happened.

Her long hair was blowing in the wind, and she looked like an angel. She was a ray of sunshine. Her skin was the color of cashews, and the glasses she wore gave her a distinguished look along with the strands of gray mingled in her hair. There wasn't a drop of makeup on her face. Her natural beauty had captivated me. Her camouflage pants and short-sleeved shirt hid her figure from me, but I could clearly tell that she was fine as hell.

Quickly turning my attention to the meat, I cleared my throat as Chad stared at me. "You good, Pop?"

"Yeah, I'm cool. Dexter's here."

Chad turned around to see him and his mother, then turned back to me with a smirk on his lips. Out of all my kids, he was the one that peeped game the quickest. He knew that she had my attention. When they got closer, Chad yelled, "What up, Dex!"

They slapped hands and hugged, then Dexter introduced his mother to Chad. She held her hand out to shake his, but I already knew what was going to happen. Chad was fun loving and considered Dexter to be his brother. Not disappointing me, he pulled her to him and hugged her tightly. Her skin reddened as she chuckled.

Dexter then brought her to me. "How you doing, Mr. Berotte?"

I shook his outstretched hand. "I'm good. How about you?"

"I'm good. This is my mother, Anissa Dent. Mama, this is Chad's father, Sheldon Berotte."

She stared right into my eyes and smiled. "It's nice to meet you, Mr. Berotte. Do you need help with anything?" she asked as she looked around.

"Nice meeting you also. No, ma'am, I don't. Thanks."

I turned back to the barbeque pit to check the sausage and boudin. I knew that it wasn't ready yet. I just needed to take my attention to anything but her. My body was reacting to her in ways I was no longer familiar with. When I lowered the lid, I was surprised to see her still standing there. Those big, dreamy eyes had me stuck. As I stared at her, her cheeks reddened, and she looked behind her for a moment, then turned back to me.

"I'm sorry, Mr. Berotte. I'm not used to going somewhere and not helping. The guys all went inside."

She seemed a little nervous, but I got that quite often. I rarely smiled, so I could understand her nervousness. "Well, Mrs. Dent, you'll have to get used to doing nothing today."

"Miss Dent, not missus."

I nodded then walked away from her while she stood there and watched me. I headed inside the house and frowned when I saw Chad watching from the window. When I walked in, he lifted his hands as I asked, "You tryna set me up?"

"Nope. That's all you, playboy."

I looked at him from the corners of my eyes as I walked to the bathroom. Almost twenty-five years and then boom. I'd given up on experiencing anything with a woman after Marie. Just the way this woman's presence had me feeling was crazy, and I didn't like it. Staring into the mirror, I rubbed my hand down my salt and pepper beard and took a deep breath, then slowly shook my head. I didn't know how I would even be in the vicinity of this woman without staring at her. Some gathering this was going to be.

Quickly making my way back outside to check the sausage and the boudin, I saw Ms. Dent taking it off the pit. I wanted to be angry, but at the same time, I thought a woman that knew her way around the barbeque pit was sexy, especially one as big as mine. When I got to her, she turned to me with a smile. "Sorry. I didn't want the food to burn. I didn't know how long you would be gone."

I didn't say a word, just took the tongs from her and resumed getting the meat off the pit. She was staring at me as I finished the job she'd started. Accepting the obvious hint I threw out there, she walked away and went sat at a table by herself. *I could have thanked her or something. Ugh.* She was invading my space, physically and mentally, and I didn't know how to handle that. Until I did, I needed her away from me. While I wasn't a friendly person, I wasn't normally this rude.

I glanced over at her again to see her sitting there with her legs crossed and her eyes closed. She looked so peaceful and serene, the opposite of me. My spirit was disturbed. Chad bumped my shoulder, catching me staring at her. "She's beautiful, huh? This is my first time meeting her, believe it or not. She keeps to herself big time, so I was surprised she came."

I didn't answer his question. I began taking the pans to the food table so people could eat. "Chad, tell Alexz to bring out the potato salad and green beans."

"I'll go help her."

He left me to arranging food on the table as Dylan walked up with some woman. "Dad, this is Ms. Ronda, Trey and Travis mama."

I nodded at her. "Nice to meet you. I'm Sheldon."

She smiled big then slowly scanned my body. This wasn't the best idea. I would have to talk to my kids when this was over. Chad said he wasn't trying to set me up, and I believed him, because Anissa wasn't paying me the least bit of attention now. She was content sitting at that table alone until Dexter sat with her.

When Chad and Alexz came out of the house arguing, I rolled my eyes. To say they were eight years apart, they argued the most.

Chad was so damn outspoken and could come off as rude and tactless at times. Alexz was so free with everything she did. She didn't care what anyone thought about the choices she made in her life, which left her wide open for Chad's ridicule. "Girl, I'll grab you by that ring in your nose and drag you all over this backyard."

"Nigga, fuck you."

"Come on, y'all. Not in front of company."

"He came at me with that energy, and I matched it!" Alexz yelled.

"So, in other words, you're having a temper tantrum and yelling, *He started it,* right?"

She huffed and rolled her eyes. "Chad, leave your sister alone."

He set the green beans on the table, then she set the potato salad next to it. My oldest, Isaiah, came out with a bowl of something and a woman in tow. I wasn't sure what it was. We didn't cook anything else. "My homeboy's mom made rice dressing," he said as he set it with the rest of the food.

I nodded my thanks to her as she smiled. We'd met briefly before. Shyrón brought out the dinner rolls, and I let everyone know that they could fix their plates. Walking out to my garage, I got the cooler of alcoholic beverages and brought it where everyone could see it, then sat in my chair, watching everyone and playing a game on my phone. This was the worst idea I could have agreed to.

Isaiah came and sat next to me. I noticed he'd been watching me since I broke up Chad and Alexz's lil fight. "You're not eating?"

"Yeah, once everyone has gotten what they wanted. I'm not really hungry right now."

"You sure you okay though? I mean, you always quiet, but you seem really zoned out right now."

"I'm okay, son."

"Yeah. We'll talk about it later."

Isaiah was the one I talked to the most. I supposed since he was the oldest, I found myself confiding in him like a friend at times. It was like he thought he was my counselor or some shit like that. He worked for the health department and often talked to different people about contraceptives and things of that nature, so I assumed he thought he was qualified to counsel me. I rolled my eyes at the thought.

As I noticed that everyone had gotten them something to eat, before I could get up, I glanced over at Ms. Dent. She was talking with Ms. Ronda and seemed to be having a great time. I couldn't get over how gorgeous she was, and still, that was bothering the hell out of me. After I'd gone to the food table and fixed my plate, I went inside to sit at the dinner table. It didn't make sense to even be outside if I wasn't going to talk to anybody. Since everyone was occupied, they wouldn't notice I'd disappeared.

3

Anissa

It was hot, and I just wanted to go home and relax. Besides a lady named Ronda, no one else was as friendly, not even the host. While he was a good-looking man, he was rude as hell. I was never the type of person that begged someone to be in their presence. I'd already tried twice with this man. I was done.

Dexter had been chilling with his friends, and they all seemed pretty cool. I was happy to meet them, although I usually kept to myself. Dexter had allowed me to do so, refusing to bring anyone into my space. After dealing with his father for years, I was so done with trying to forge relationships with people. I had enough life interruptions for two lifetimes. I was good on that.

The food was good though. Had it not been for me, the damn sausage and boudin would have burned. I rolled my eyes as I thought about his rude ass. However, I tried not to judge him. Maybe he was going through something that kept him from socializing with people. He hadn't talked to anyone, so I didn't take his attitude personally.

As I looked around, I noticed that he was no longer outside. Dexter had to know that I wasn't really enjoying myself. I tried hard to be social, but I was done trying. Most of the parents that were here didn't seem to want to be. *Not even the one who lived here.* I crossed my legs and pulled up the latest book in my kindle and began reading.

It seemed like as soon as I began to really fall into the storyline, I was interrupted. "Did Chad's dad leave?"

I looked over to see Ronda was back. "I don't know. He seemed to have disappeared. I gather that this isn't really his thing."

"Right. My sons said that he's been that way since his wife died nearly twenty-five years ago... extremely withdrawn and nonchalant. They've been friends with Isaiah, his oldest son, for at least twenty-three years, since they were in fifth or sixth grade. This is my first time officially meeting him though. I've seen him around, but we've never spoken. I feel sorry for him in a way. That's a man that was dedicated to his wife."

I thought about what she said, and I realized my thoughts about not judging him were spot on. While my ex-husband wasn't dead, I knew what it meant to grieve. The man I married had died when his mother died, and I gave up on him being resurrected. "That's sad," I responded.

"Yeah. Well, I'm gonna go. I would much rather be in front of my TV at this point. It was nice meeting you."

"I hear you. It was nice meeting you too."

I glanced over at the food table to see the lids were all over the place. I went to the table and began covering the food to keep the flies out of it. This sitting still was about to drive me insane. The music was decent, but like Ronda, I would much rather be at home in my own space, relaxing. I supposed my workout earlier didn't help matters. My body was still aching.

As I tightened the foil around the pans, I took it upon myself to take them in the house. No one seemed to be getting seconds. When I walked through the door, I noticed Mr. Berotte sitting at the kitchen table. I didn't look at him for long, because I didn't want him to think I was invading his space. I could tell he didn't want to be bothered, and I was more than cool with that, although, his eyes had heated me up like I was standing in front of a space heater in the wintertime. He'd caressed every inch of my body when he first saw me. Knowing what I now know, maybe he felt guilty about that. His rough voice had turned me on even more. It was probably best he pushed me away from him. He wasn't ready to move on from his deceased wife's memory, and I probably wasn't ready to entertain anyone else either.

I quickly made my way out of the door to get the rest of the food. All the rice dressing, dinner rolls, boudin, and potato salad were gone. There were only a couple of steaks and pork chops left. If he didn't say anything to me, I would organize it. It just wasn't like me to partake at someone's house without bringing a dish and not at least cleaning up afterward. I walked back inside the house to see he was no longer seated at the table.

I took the tongs from the pan and put all the meat into one then tore off a fresh sheet of foil to wrap it with. As I was grabbing the empty pans to put in the sink, I nearly ran into Mr. Berotte. I didn't hear him come into the kitchen. "What are you doing?" he asked with a hint of annoyance in his tone.

"I was bringing the food in the house before the flies had their way with it. Then I decided to combine the meat to lessen the dishes you would have in your fridge. I'm just trying to do my part, since I didn't contribute to the meal."

"I told you earlier that I had it. That hasn't changed."

I stared at him as I willed myself to calm down. I put the pans back down on the table and lifted my hands. "Fine. Handle it by yourself then. Enjoy the rest of your day, Mr. Berotte."

I walked out of the house, leaving him standing there. Even after what Ronda had told me, I still got angry. We were grown ass individuals. He didn't have to be rude. When I walked out of the door, I saw

Dexter clowning around with his friends. I walked right over to them and said, "Can you take me home? Sorry to interrupt your good time."

He smiled tightly. "Yeah. No problem."

"Nice meeting you, fellas."

"You too, Ms. Dent," they said almost in unison.

When we got to the car and I slammed the door before Dexter could close it, he frowned and went to his side to get in. Once he got in, he asked, "You okay?"

"Mr. Berotte is a jackass. I don't care what issues I was dealing with, I was never rude to people, especially not someone who was trying to help me. You don't have to ever worry about me coming back over here."

"I apologize, Ma. Chad thinks he's feeling you though."

"We aren't kids, DJ. He doesn't have to be rude to me if he likes me."

He chuckled. "He's not a friendly person. He has to come around in his time, not because someone is trying to force him to."

"I wasn't bothering that man. I was being nice and bringing the food in the house. He approached me with his ugly attitude. I tried not to take it personally, but it was hard not to, especially when one of the ladies brought rice dressing and he told her thank you. He wasn't rude to her."

"I don't know, Ma. I'm sorry for subjecting you to that. At least you met Ms. Ronda."

"We didn't trade numbers or anything. She was just someone to talk to while I was there."

I folded my arms and looked out of the window. I didn't know why I was so pissed. That man shouldn't have been affecting me the way he was. He was way too fine to be that damn rude though. I would have had to be blind not to notice how in shape he was. That gray beard needed moisturizing, and I had plenty of it on deck until he venomously attacked me for no reason. The sugar in me quickly turned to salt.

I gave him three chances to come correct. Three! The first time, he lifted the lid of his barbeque pit, in my face, then walked away from me like I wasn't there. The second time, he snatched the tongs from me when I was only trying to help. Then the third time, that was it. He might as well had told me to leave because that was the message I got. I wasn't up for being somewhere I wasn't wanted. I barely wanted to be there in the first place, but I was trying to make the best of the situation.

When we got to my apartment, I hopped out of Dexter's car then walked around to the driver door where he was trying to get out. "Go back to your friends and have a good time, baby. Thank you for trying to get me out of the house."

I kissed his cheek as he smiled at me then watched me until I'd gotten inside my apartment. Once inside, I went straight to my bathroom. It was hot as hell, and I was more than sure I smelled like outside. After starting the shower, my mind couldn't help but to go back to Sheldon Berotte. I was trying to figure out why he was the way he was and what I could have done differently. *I didn't do anything wrong.*

That was my issue with Dexter... my ex-husband. I was a fixer. When something wasn't right, I tried to fix it. Sometimes things had to fix themselves without my interference, and other times, I needed to accept that things wouldn't change unless the other person wanted them to. After going to the kitchen and grabbing a bottle of water, I went to my room to disrobe and take a shower. I supposed it would be a Lifetime movie sort of night.

※

THE KNOCKING AT THE DOOR CAUGHT ME OFF GUARD. I NEVER really had company, and my sons usually called ahead to let me know they were coming by. Thoughts of Dexter finding out where I lived began running through my mind. I turned off the TV and eased off the couch, trying to be as quiet as possible. When I got to the door and saw DJ and his friend Chad, I breathed out a sigh of relief. While he'd never brought Chad to my place, I was okay with it versus who I thought it was.

I opened the door, and he smiled. "I'm sorry for popping up on you, Ma."

"It's okay, DJ. Y'all come in."

After closing the door, I realized they were holding a to-go container. Pretending not to see it, I went back to the couch. "I wanted to bring you some barbeque for later if you got hungry again," Chad said.

"Thank you. I appreciate that."

They talked quietly in the kitchen. I knew they were here for more than that. DJ could have brought that on his way home and not made a special trip here. It wasn't like I was hungry now, although the smell of it had me wanting to heat it up anyway. I turned the TV back on and pulled my blanket over me. I was already ready for bed, and it was only seven o'clock. My hair was wrapped, and I had on my pajamas. Chad probably thought I was an old maid, but I didn't care.

When they rejoined me, they just stood over me. I frowned as I sat up on the sofa and paused the movie again. "What?"

"Umm... Mr. Berotte wanted us to apologize to you. He said you were triggering him."

I frowned harder. "Triggering him?"

"Your personality is a lot like my mom's personality was... always trying to help, accommodating, and sweet. I was only seven, almost eight, when she died, but I've held on to memories of her. She catered to my dad like he was her king. You reminded him of her by trying to help so much."

I brought my hand to my chest as I felt my heart practically sink to my feet. I could sympathize with him on that, but after a moment, I stared back up at them. "So why didn't he call and apologize for himself? You could have called me from your phone, DJ, and he could have apologized. We're grown, and I don't have time for childish behavior. Tell him apology accepted. Now bye."

DJ and Chad chuckled like something was funny. I was serious as a heart attack. Sheldon Berotte could clearly tell what type of woman I was. He should have known that he could come to me like a man and say what he had to say. I rolled my eyes as DJ said, "We'll be sure to relay the message. So I guess you okay with us giving him your phone number?"

"What?"

"You said he could call you and say all that shit to you himself," DJ responded.

"I also said you could have called from your phone, and he could have talked to me."

"Ms. Dent, no disrespect, but that ain't gon' fly with Sheldon Berotte. He way too private to let us hear that type of conversation. I haven't seen his sensitive side since my sister was a lil girl and she'd fallen from the monkey bars at the park. So, if you want to hear the apology from him, we'd have to give him your number."

"I suppose you came along to be his mouthpiece."

Chad chuckled. "Naw. He would kill me if he knew I was telling you all this. I just hate seeing him so angry all the time. You sparked something in him, something that's been dormant for a long time. I want to see him really live again."

"You sound like DJ," I said softly. He often said that to me... wanting me to really live again and not be afraid of loving someone again. "Give it to him. Let him know I won't accept his apology until I hear it from him."

"You feeling him too, Ma, I can see it, but both of y'all are so afraid of experiencing something meaningful again. Hopefully, y'all won't be so stubborn if he calls."

I covered myself back up and started my movie. I couldn't have this conversation with them. DJ leaned over and kissed my cheek. "I love you, Ma."

"Love you too."

When they walked out, I exhaled my nerves. I couldn't believe I told him that it was okay to give that man my number. *What if he called tonight? What if he didn't call at all? Why did I care?* My thoughts were driving me insane. The movie was going, and I hadn't seen or heard a thing. I turned the TV off and paced in my front room then went to the kitchen to eat some comfort food. *Sheldon's barbeque.*

4

Sheldon

"She said she ain't accepting that lame ass apology until you call her yourself."

I frowned. "She said it like that?"

Dexter laughed then pushed Chad's stupid ass. "My mama would never say no shit like that. She did say that she wanted to hear the apology from you, but she didn't say it like that, nor did she say lame ass."

They laughed, making fun of this situation. I didn't know why I even got their asses involved. *Chad of all people.* That fool didn't have a serious bone in his body. However, they were my only way to her. I'd let my thoughts of Marie cause me to treat her badly. That woman... Anissa Dent... she reminded me so much of Marie. When she came inside the house, I was already in my damn feelings. I knew she'd seen me, but to avoid my attitude, she ignored me. That irritated me more.

She couldn't do anything right, and I knew it was because I was extremely attracted to her. "Can you put her number in my phone?" I asked Dexter.

"Yes, sir. Her name is Anissa Dent."

Oh, I remember her name. Her name was seared into my mental like the brand on Chad's arm when he pledged Omega Psi Phi. When he gave my phone back to me, I stared at it for a moment, trying to decide if I would call her tonight or wait until tomorrow. I looked up at him and asked, "Does she work? I mean, if I called during the day tomorrow, would I disrupt her workday?"

"Naw. She's been retired for a month or so now."

"Okay."

That meant she could be just as free as me and come and go as she pleased. They finally turned their attention away from me. Everyone else had left already. Once Anissa left, I'd gone back outside and started cleaning up, feeling like an asshole. Retreating to my bedroom, I sat on a chair I had positioned in the corner and stared at my phone, deciding to just make the damn call. It rang twice, and as I was preparing to end the call at the third ring, she answered. "Hello?"

Her voice was soft and sweet like it was at the barbeque... just like Marie's had been. I cleared my throat and said, "Hello, Ms. Dent. This is Sheldon. I was calling to apologize for my behavior, including sending an apology through our sons."

I didn't want to get that personal with her and offer her an explanation, although I felt like I owed her one. She remained quiet for a moment, as if waiting for me to continue. When I didn't, she said, "Okay. Apology accepted. Have a good night."

"Ms. Dent," I said, not really wanting to let go of her voice, but I didn't have a clue what to say.

"Yes?"

When I remained quiet, she took a deep breath. "Well, you know my name is Anissa Dent. I'm fifty-three years old. I retired from the post office a month ago. I have two sons, and I've been divorced for fifteen years. Tell me about yourself, Mr. Berotte."

"Well, umm... for starters, you can call me Sheldon. I'm a widower. My wife died giving birth to my twenty-four-year-old daughter. All five of my kids were under the age of ten when that happened. I quit my job and raised them alone. I had help every now and then from her parents, but not a lot since they lived a couple of hours away."

I took a deep breath and rubbed my hand down my face. "Ms. Dent... I mean, Anissa. You're so kind, and you reminded me of Marie for a moment. You don't look like her, but she was always willing to help. It was like it pained her to sit still and watch other people work. That about you reminded me of her. But the part that stunned me the most was the fact that you are the first woman to really catch my attention since she's been gone."

I slid my hand down my face. I couldn't believe I said all that to her. She was quiet, but I could clearly hear her breathing. Curiosity of what she would say kept me on the phone because the thought of hanging up and never talking to her again had crossed my mind. Finally, she responded. "I don't know whether to apologize or be flattered."

Her voice was so soft. I didn't know if she was talking to me or herself, but I found myself responding anyway. "You can't apologize for being you," I said just as softly. *What was I doing?* "Well, I'm sorry to take up your time, Anissa. I just wanted to give you what you asked for... an 'I'm sorry' straight from me."

"Thank you. All is forgiven. Goodnight."

I ended the call and immediately wanted to call her back. Her voice had pulled me in, and I just wanted to listen to her talk all night. I didn't understand how I'd gone damn near twenty-five years without any attraction to a woman, then like dynamite, she exploded onto my scene. The crazy part was that Dexter and Chad had been friends for years. How I had never seen her before now was a mystery to me.

Standing, I went to the bathroom and started the shower. Before I could get in, my phone rang. When I went to it, I was surprised to see Anissa calling me back. I hesitated for a moment, but I answered. "Hello?"

"I'm sorry for disturbing you, but I was wondering... umm. I feel weird all of a sudden. Ugh!"

"Would you like to go to a late dinner, Anissa?"

She was quiet for a moment, and I didn't know what had gotten into me. *I was asking a woman out! What the fuck?* "How about drinks instead? I'm not really hungry," she responded.

"Sounds like a plan. I'm about to shower. Text me your address, and I'll come pick you up."

"O-okay."

When I ended the call, I couldn't believe I'd done that, but my heart felt light as hell. Getting in the shower, I washed up quickly then got out and got dressed. After spraying on some cologne and putting on my chain, diamond studs, and watch, I grabbed my phone to see Anissa's text, then headed out of the room. When I got to the kitchen and saw Chad was still here, rummaging through my fridge while he was on the phone, I silently cursed.

He turned to me as he ended his phone call, and a smirk made its way to his lips. Before he could open his mouth, I said, "Shut up. I don't even want to hear your mouth right now. Come on so I can lock up. Go to your own place."

"I can't believe you going out. For the first time in a while, I ain't have shit to do. Fine. I'll go home." He walked out, and I locked the door. As he watched me walk to my car, he said, "Tell Ms. Dent I said what's up."

I often wondered where I went wrong raising that fool. He was bigger and taller than me, but he was a big ass clown most times. I thought working at the prison would have leveled him out some, but he got worse. Once I was inside of my car, I texted Anissa, letting her know that I was on my way and should be at her apartment in fifteen minutes. She quickly responded, informing me she would be ready.

This was crazy. I couldn't believe I was actually doing this. As I drove to her complex, my phone rang. When I saw it was Chad, I rolled my eyes then answered. "What?"

"You ain't gotta be all salty with me. Where y'all going?"

"Get drinks."

"Call an Uber if you need one... meaning me. It's a first date, but if she wanna go all the way—"

I ended the call on his stupidness. It had been a while since I'd been on an actual date, but I supposed that was what this was. *Not really.* I didn't know what the hell this was. I just knew that I wanted to get to know her. I wasn't even sure why she'd called back, but it had to be along the lines of asking me out or something.

When the phone rang again, I ignored it. I wasn't about to be bothered with Chad and his foolishness tonight. The closer I got to her place, the more nervous I became. I wasn't sure why she'd been divorced or how she was living her life since her divorce, but besides her beauty and similar characteristics to Marie, something more was pulling me in her direction.

My mind raced until I got to her place. As I parked, I took a deep breath, something I'd been seeming to do all night to settle my nerves, then got out of the car. After taking only one step toward her apartment, she stepped outside. She'd really been waiting for me. Instead of walking to meet her, I walked to the other side of my car so I could open the door. Once she got to me, she smiled. I could tell that she was just as nervous as I was.

"Hi, Sheldon."

"Hey, Anissa."

I opened the door for her, and she slid inside. She looked so beautiful in her jeans, heels, and fitted shirt. Since it was a Dallas Cowboys shirt, I took it that she was a fan. That was good news since I was too. When I got inside, I turned to her. Her dreamy eyes landed on mine, and she offered me a closed lip smile. I wasn't really the type to smile unless I was amused or laughing, so I didn't. "You look beautiful," I offered.

Once again, she didn't wear makeup, but she did have on lip gloss. I supposed that just wasn't her thing. I was cool with that. Her hair, though... it was so beautiful. While I wanted to touch it, I didn't know how she would feel about that just yet.

She quickly scanned my body, adorned in blue jeans, a polo style shirt, and Sperrys. "Thank you. You look nice yourself. So where are we going?"

"Pour 09. You ever been there?"

"No. You?"

"Nope."

She chuckled, and just the sound of that had my lips curling upward a bit. Before I drove off, I asked, "What were you going to ask me when you called back?"

"I really don't know. I just didn't want to stop talking to you so soon."

I nodded. She felt the same pull that I did, and it seemed that she wasn't really sure how to handle it either. Taking off from my parking spot, I made my way to Pour 09, which was only a few minutes from where she lived, near Walmart. Glancing at her repeatedly, I could see that she was enjoying the R&B music. "I take it you like music."

"I love it. It's the perfect space filler when you either don't feel like talking or don't know what to say. I'm quiet sometimes, especially since I haven't been out with a man in a long time."

"What's a long time?"

"Over sixteen years."

It seemed we were practically the same person. I wondered if she was pining after her ex. I was never one to be shy about what I wanted to know, so I asked, "Why?"

She shrugged her shoulders, then said, "Like you, I just haven't met anyone to catch my interest. My divorce was a turbulent one, so I wasn't in a hurry to meet anyone."

"I understand. How long were you married?"

"Nearly twenty years. We got married right after I graduated high school. He went to the military and wanted me to move away with him. He'd already been in for two years when I graduated. We only stayed gone two or three years. Once his time was up, he chose not to reenlist. We moved back home and both started working for the post office."

"If you don't mind me asking, what went wrong?"

I could see her fidget a bit, in my peripheral, then look out of the window. Surely this conversation couldn't be that difficult if they'd been divorced for so long. She turned back to me and swallowed hard. "When his mom died, he lost it. She was the only parent he knew, and they were extremely close. I believed that was why he didn't reenlist, because it was killing him to be away from her. He started drinking a lot, popping pills, doing anything to dull the pain. After a while, I knew that I couldn't keep my boys in that toxic environment."

"Where is he now?"

"I don't know. I haven't seen him in a year and a half. He was a drug addict, popping up on me all the time. DJ convinced me that I needed a fresh start. I sold my house and moved into an apartment. He doesn't know where I live."

That was some shit right there. He was torturing her, but it seemed like she still loved him. Through all that bullshit, she still cared. "That had to be hard. I mean to watch someone you love decline and not be able to do anything to stop it," I said as I turned in the parking lot.

"Extremely hard."

She was in her feelings now, and I hated that I'd even asked. I was impressed with how she willingly answered my questions though. It seemed she was grieving just as I was, except she was trying to overcome the devastation of losing the man she'd married to the streets.

Without another word, I got out of the car and walked around to open her door, only to see that she'd already gotten out. She was used to doing for herself. I preferred opening doors for a woman, especially one I was interested in. I was always that way with Marie. She never objected to that. We were young though. I didn't say anything to Anissa regarding that. Instead, I reached for her hand.

She hesitantly slid her hand in mine as I said, "Let's go see what this is about."

5

Anissa

I sat here on the outdoor, second-level patio, nursing on a margarita on the rocks, wishing that I wouldn't have talked about Dexter. Thinking or speaking of him could put a damper on any mood or situation. While I knew Sheldon was just trying to get to know me, I should have reserved that conversation for another time. I glanced over at him as he drank his scotch. The man was the epitome of the word zaddy.

I was in total shock that he'd called as quickly as he did. Maybe he wasn't as standoffish as he seemed. He did seem just as nervous as I was though. I was extremely nervous and didn't understand how I was so comfortable getting into the car of a man I'd just met and wasn't initially impressed with. Allowing him to come to my place and pick me up didn't even feel weird to me. That alone was weird in itself.

Glancing at him again, I noticed he was staring at the TV. It didn't really seem like he was watching it. I nervously slid my hand over his. This wasn't my scene. I didn't really like going out. When he glanced at me, I knew that, somehow, he knew what I was thinking.

He got the bartender's attention and paid for our drinks. "This ain't my scene either," he said. "I just didn't know how comfortable you would be with me alone in one of our houses."

"Our sons are friends. I doubt that either of us could get away with much."

He smiled slightly. "Chad had the nerve to try to tell me how to behave on a date."

I chuckled. "DJ did the same when I called to let him know that I was going out. He thinks he's my parent now."

"Same with my five." He slowly shook his head then threw his drink back. "Whenever you're ready, so am I."

I did the same to my margarita, but just as I was about to stand, these people had the nerve to play "The One" by Cee-Lo. That used to be my jam! That was the whole vibe for 2004 for me. When I remained seated and started vibing, putting my finger in the air because I was the one, I could see the look of amusement on Sheldon's face. "I'm sorry, but this is my song."

Before long, I'd forgotten anyone was there and stood from my seat to dance. When I looked up, there were a couple of women that had joined me. Apparently, the person in control of the music was happy that we were enjoying ourselves, because he put on another jam by Anthony Hamilton and Lil Jon. When I saw Sheldon laugh, I knew that he was enjoying himself. The man didn't smile for nothing.

Making my way to him, I pulled him from his seat and began dancing again. Surprisingly, he spun me around and wrapped his arms around my waist. We swayed to the beat of the music. Feeling him that close to me felt amazing. He didn't strike me as the type to really dance, but I supposed I was wrong. When I heard him sing along with Anthony Hamilton, *Alright, I'm ready*, I was in shock. However, it seemed he was saying that directly to me.

His embrace got a little tighter, and as we grooved, I couldn't help but to close my eyes. I inhaled his scent and relaxed in what I was feeling. This was foreign to me, and I was happy to feel again. Until now, it was like I'd been numb all these years to these types of feelings. I just felt good. As the song ended, I turned to him. Childish Gambino was next. I liked "Redbone", but it wasn't a song I needed to dance to. Sheldon felt differently.

He pulled me back to him as he stared in my eyes. This was intense. I slid my hands up his chest to his shoulders, and when I looked back up at him, he gently kissed my lips. My body practically melted, threatening to leak through the cracks in the wooden floor to the first level. However, the shock of what he'd done caused him to pull away from me.

I grabbed his hand to stop him. When he turned back to me, his face was hard. "We can go."

I quickly nodded and grabbed my purse, following behind him. I didn't understand what was so bad about what happened. My soul was light, and for the first time in sixteen years, I wanted to be with a man. When we got downstairs and had left the place, I grabbed his hand again. "Sheldon. Wait." He stopped walking and turned to me. "What's wrong? Did I do something wrong?"

He took a deep breath and slid his free hand down his face. Turning back toward the car, he resumed walking. When he got to the passenger side, he remained still. He didn't open the door, just stood there staring at it. His grief was making him feel guilty about what he was feeling between us. Before I could say anything, he turned back to me and pulled me close to him. I slid my arms around his waist and laid against him.

It just felt like he needed comforting. We both seemed to be warring with our pasts, and maybe we were supposed to be here for one another. "I'm sorry, Anissa."

"No apology needed. Letting go is hard. I know firsthand."

I lifted my head to look at him only to find him staring at me. He lowered his head slightly and kissed my forehead, then turned and opened the door for me. Getting inside, I felt like depression and guilt were looming over me. I couldn't have that. Once he dropped me home, I would have to meditate big time. I wasn't sure if I was strong enough for him to not suck me in and have me feeling like he did.

When he got in the car, he grabbed my hand. "I didn't mean to ruin the good time we were having. I was enjoying myself."

"I was too."

I gave his hand a squeeze, and I could see that he was really warring with his mind. Slowly, I lifted my hand and placed it on his cheek, then ran my fingers through his nearly white beard. He closed his eyes and accepted my way of soothing him. When he released a low moan, the goosebumps popped up on my skin. He wanted to be whole. I could feel that about him. He just didn't know how to stop feeling guilty about it.

When he opened his eyes, he pulled me close and gently kissed my lips. Just like before, it had me melting in my seat. He stared at me for a moment then said in his raspy voice, "Thank you."

Although I wasn't quite sure what he was thanking me for exactly, I had a clue. I gave him a tight smile and nodded. He started the car, and we headed back to my place. Trying to lighten the mood, I said, "So 'Redbone' must be your jam, like that Cee-Lo joint was mine."

He chuckled. "Yeah. That Anthony Hamilton jams, too, the entire album."

"It does. I see we have that in common. Good music is my weakness. I'm not shy, but I'm somewhat reserved until something pulls me out of it."

"Well, I'm glad that song came on. I'm not shy either, but I'm extremely reserved and guarded. I haven't been out like this in a long ass time. Just the fact that you were able to pull me from a low place speaks volumes to me. If I can get over the guilt I feel because of that, I'll be doing good."

I squeezed his hand as we continued to my apartment. I liked how he seemed so open with me. It was the total opposite of what he gave me earlier. When we got to my apartment complex and he parked, I turned to him. "Would you like to come in?"

He didn't answer me verbally, but when he killed his engine, I knew he would be coming inside. Just as I reached for the door handle, he grabbed my hand. "Anissa, chill out. I got the door."

I sat back in my seat, and a smile fell on my lips. To me, this confirmed that this was a date. We weren't just hanging out, trying to get to know one another as friends. While I knew it was a respect thing, most of the guys I was cool with in the past never opened doors for me. It was like I was one of the fellas. When he opened the door, he grabbed my hand and helped me from my seat. "Thank you."

He followed me to my door, and I got nervous... not that he would do anything to me, but just the fact I would be alone with a man who I was interested in. Once we were inside, I turned to him. "Would you like a drink? I have wine, water, and DJ left a couple of beers in the fridge."

"A bottle of water is good. Thanks."

I nodded then headed to the kitchen. Before I could get our drinks, I started some music. As I poured my wine, Sevyn Streeter began playing through my speaker. I hadn't had a chance to finish listening to the album, so I let it play. As I sat, I realized what she was saying. When I heard, *Don't let the pussy go to waste,* my face heated up tremendously. I hurriedly found something else to listen to.

After lowering the volume, I handed Sheldon his water. He looked like he wanted to laugh though. "Something funny?" I asked as I put my hand on my hip.

He chuckled. "Yeah. We grown. If you a freak, then you a freak. No apologies. Ain't that what the song say?"

I gave him the side eye as he laughed more. "I hadn't heard that song yet. I was listening to her album earlier, thank you very much."

I sat next to him and practically guzzled my wine. He laughed so hard. My embarrassment was at an all-time high though. He reached out and touched the hair on my shoulder. When he scooted closer to me, I leaned into him a bit. "I love your hair. It's beautiful."

"Thank you. I've thought about cutting it several times."
"Why?"
"Just for something different."

He scanned me from head to toe then continued playing in my hair. My body was heating internally, and I just hoped it wasn't visible from the outside. Sheldon wasn't saying much of anything, but he seemed at peace in the quietness. He put his arm around me and laid his head against mine. I reached over and grabbed his other hand. I just wanted to hold it, but when he wrapped it around me, I stared up into his eyes.

I was mesmerized by the passion I saw in them. I didn't know this man, but I could clearly see he needed the comfort my presence was giving him. I gently kissed his lips, and he rested his forehead against mine. "You aren't going to believe this shit, but I haven't been with a woman in twenty-five years... in no way."

"I haven't been with a man since I divorced my husband. He's the only man I've been with in every way... no one else. That's why this seems so special. I mean... the way we seem to be drawn to one another. We have so much in common until it's somewhat scary. But maybe that barbeque was supposed to happen, if for nothing more than for us to meet."

He brought his lips to mine again, but he wasn't so quick to pull away this time. He allowed it to linger. When he did pull away, he said, "It feels like I've known you for a long time."

"Same here."

He slowly pulled away from me and drank some of his water. I took that opportunity to change the conversation. "So what was it like raising a little girl? I always wanted a daughter."

"It was work. I created a monster. She's so spoiled." He paused to laugh. "Her brothers spoiled her too. Although she can't get along with Chad to save her life, I think she secretly likes it that way. He's the only one that she fights with. He's the only one that really fights back. She's smart and responsible though."

"That's good. My boys turned out to be responsible as well,

despite everything." My phone began ringing, and I slightly rolled my eyes. "I'm pretty sure that's one of them now."

I grabbed my phone from the table to see that my youngest son, Jamel, was calling. I silenced the call and texted him to say I would call him back. "Sorry. If I didn't say something, he would have kept calling, then would have had DJ coming to see about me."

"Sounds like we're in the same boat. Our kids worry about us."

"Yeah, but they think because I would rather stay to myself that I'm depressed. While I once was, I am no longer. I'm just content with having peace."

"If I'm alone and still for too long, I start sinking. That's why I keep busy and take naps. Maybe I need to see a grief counselor. I talk to my oldest son, Isaiah, at times, but there are things that I don't feel comfortable sharing with him."

"Seeing a counselor won't hurt, that's for sure. I talked to one, but until I was ready to let go of Dexter, it wasn't helping. I constantly tried to get him help. It wasn't until he'd drained us dry and practically sold everything in the house that I divorced him. Even after that, when he'd convince me he was clean, I would allow him to come back. That happened twice. It was like I divorced him three times. But he's the only man I've ever known... the only man I ever loved."

I took a deep breath then turned to Sheldon as he went back to playing in my hair. The way he stared at me told me that he was about to lay something heavy on me, and I was prepared to handle it.

"You're a good woman, Anissa. That's for sure." He lowered his gaze for a moment then looked back up at me. "Marie wasn't my first, but she was my last and my only love. Sometimes I feel less of a man because I haven't been with a woman in so long. I had kids to raise, but I don't know what the excuse has been for the past six years. Alexz graduated high school six years ago, and she fell off my dime two years ago when she graduated college and got a job."

"There's no shame in that, Sheldon. It's admirable."

"Today, I realized that my heart is ready. My mind is crucifying me though. I want to get to know everything about you. I want to know love again. Just the fact that I'm able to share that with you lets me know just how special you are."

He gently rubbed my cheek with the back of his hand. Closing my eyes and leaning into his touch came like second nature to me. Our spirits had already connected. It was fast. However, I believed our spirits sensed the familiarity in each other. When he withdrew his hand, I opened my eyes. "Listen. I uhh... I don't mean this in a sexual way, but..."

I couldn't verbalize what I wanted to say to him. It wouldn't come out. Suddenly, I became nervous all over again. I looked away from him, but he gently put his fingers to my chin and turned my head back to him. "I'd love to stay tonight."

My eyes widened. I didn't know how he knew that was what I wanted to say. I wanted to offer him what Angela Bassett offered Wesley Snipes in *Waiting to Exhale* in that hotel room. He seemed to need that, and truth was, I needed it too. I stood, and he did so as well, then I led him to my bedroom. After taking off our shoes, we got in bed fully clothed. I turned my back to him, and he wrapped his arms around me. "Thank you, Anissa. I needed this."

He kissed my cheek and exhaled as I relaxed in his embrace, knowing that this felt just right.

6

Sheldon

"I can't believe you're just getting home. When I got here and didn't see your car, I thought that maybe you had gone to the store," Isaiah said.

I shook my head slowly. He didn't know where I'd been, and I was grateful that fool Chad wasn't the one to greet me when I got here.

Last night was so amazing. I didn't want to leave Anissa this morning. She wanted to go to church, and since I wasn't prepared, I came home. I stayed until the last minute, leaving at the same time she did. I didn't get here until 10:45. Had she not been going to church, I would probably still be with her.

She brought peace to my soul. I wasn't willing to admit that I was tortured until after meeting her. I thought I had a handle on things.

However, when my body craved her, I knew I didn't. Guilt was coursing through me something fierce. As I held her in my arms, my dick got hard. I knew she had to have felt it, but she didn't acknowledge it.

I sat on my barstool, and Isaiah joined me after setting the pack of beef meat on the countertop.

"I went out for drinks with Dexter's mom."

"Dexter? Chad's friend, DJ?"

"Yeah. Something about her attracts me. Her spirit is so genuine and sweet. We ended up going back to her place, and I'm just getting home."

His eyebrows shot up, and I knew he was thinking that I slept with her. I shook my head and held my hand up as he was about to ask the question. "We didn't have sex. She offered me peace... intimacy... solace. I held her all night. Our clothes never came off, son."

"Wow. That's... umm... I don't have any words for it."

"It was definitely spiritual. I'm extremely attracted to her, and I know she's attracted to me too. We experienced a few kisses... nothing sexual or nasty, but they were just as passionate. My guilt almost consumed me, but my spirit wouldn't allow me to pull away from her. When I tried, within minutes, I was explaining to her what happened. She wasn't judgmental, and she was very understanding because she's been through a similar experience. We couldn't be more alike. We were supposed to meet and destined to be in this very place we're in. I don't know where this will lead, but I know that I want to see her again."

"Damn. That's powerful, Dad. I'm happy for you. I feel like this is what you've been needing. I'm just glad you were receptive to it."

"I didn't have a choice. The way I ignored her and was rude to her while she was here nagged at me so bad. My soul wouldn't allow me to push her away."

He patted my back and slowly shook his head. "It almost sounds like you love her. That was beautiful. I want something like that. I'm ready to start a family. I just haven't met the woman I want to take a leap with yet." He glanced at the meat he set on the countertop. "Let me start on these beef tips before everybody else gets here."

I nodded then retreated to my bedroom to take a shower before the others got here asking questions. I woke up a couple of times last night, and I still couldn't believe I was somewhere other than my own home. Anissa seemed so innocent to me, even after that song came on. She was so red. Just thinking about it had me chuckling. I wished I could have gone to church with her because I couldn't stop thinking about her.

After taking a shower and getting dressed, I headed back toward the kitchen to help Isaiah, but before I could get there, I heard my second oldest in there tripping. "That nigga did what? I know you lying."

"Chad, cool out."

"Oh, I'm happy as hell, Zay. You ain't gotta tell me to cool out. I just can't believe it. So they fucked?"

"Naw."

"Who fucked?"

I recognized that voice as being Dylan. He was the youngest boy. I figured I had better get in there before they started making up their own story. The moment I walked into the kitchen, all talking ceased, and Chad stared at me with a stupid grin on his face. "Good morning," I said to them.

"Mm hmm. So instead of calling your personal Uber, you just stayed over? I thought you were out of touch, but clearly, you still on game," Chad said as he crossed his arms over his chest.

"Shut up, Chad," I said before he could continue.

Dylan placed his hand on my shoulder. He was the one who looked the most like me. While he was lowkey, he was the nastiest. He didn't think I knew that though. Going to the grocery store in gray sweats was a stunt he pulled quite often. I knew that all my boys were blessed. They couldn't help it. Their old man was blessed beyond measure too. So those gray sweats didn't hide a damn thing.

"Dad, you were with someone last night?"

"Yeah, for drinks. Nothing else happened, so don't let Chad fill your head with his foolishness."

"Ask him what time he got home, Dylan," Chad said.

Dylan looked back at him then turned back to me, his eyebrows hiked up in a questioning manner. "About thirty minutes ago," I mumbled.

"See! I wanna be like you when I grow up!" Chad said and laughed.

I slowly shook my head as Dylan stood there in shock. "Yoooo! Dad, you stayed all night, and nothing happened?" he asked.

"No, son. We talked, then I held her until we both went to sleep. There's more to being with a woman than just having sex. Don't listen to Chad. I don't know where I went wrong with that fool. I promise, he knocks down my level of pride with how y'all turned out every time."

He chuckled then shook my hand as Chad said, "Don't let Dylan fool you. He worse than me. I just don't hide shit."

Dylan pushed him and said, "Ain't nobody hiding, nigga. I just keep my shit to myself."

I slowly shook my head as I glanced at Isaiah adding green beans and potatoes to the pot. Shyrón and Alexz must have been sleeping in since they weren't here yet. I stood from my seat and started a pot of rice since Chad and Dylan had retreated to the family room and turned on the TV. When I glanced at Isaiah, I noticed he was just staring off into space. When I brought my hand to his shoulder, he flinched. "Son, you good?"

"I'm okay. I'm just thinking about this young girl that came into my office. Her mom brought her to the health department when she found out she was sexually active. Just from looking in her eyes, it seems like there's more to the story. She's so withdrawn. She doesn't really fit the type of girl that's just rebelling."

"Well, if it's nagging at you this much, maybe it's worth looking into."

"Yeah, but I don't wanna make accusations without the facts. She won't give me the facts as long as her mother is there. I'm a male counselor wanting to speak to a teenaged girl alone. How am I supposed to make that happen without looking suspect myself?"

"And David was a midget compared to Goliath. What's your point? You'll figure out something."

"You right. You right," he reiterated while nodding. "It's gon' be an uphill battle, but I know I got this."

I smiled as I patted his back. Out of all my children, Isaiah was the one that inherited his mother's heart. While Chad could sniff out bullshit, Isaiah could feel sincerity and a genuine spirit. He also thrived on helping a person find their happy place. He picked the perfect career that nurtured his gifts. Before I could retreat to the den with the other two, Alexz walked through the door. "Hey, baby."

"Hey, Daddy."

"Oooh. That sounded dry."

"Sorry. I'm so tired," she said as she set a pan of cornbread on the countertop. "I was up late trying to decide what's next for me."

"What do you mean?"

"Well... I'm seeing someone. He wanted to come to the barbeque yesterday, but I wasn't ready to introduce him to y'all yet. I need to feel him out just a little bit more first. You know y'all don't take it easy on anybody wanting to be with me."

"That shows if he's man enough, Alexz. If he can't deal with your father and brothers, then he ain't the one," Isaiah said, causing Alexz to huff.

"He has a point. It's not like we attack your prospects. We just ask questions."

"Lots of damn questions. I just need more time."

"So what were you trying to decide then? You seem pretty sound in that decision."

"Yeah, but I'm not as sound in exactly how I feel about him. I mean, I like him, maybe even love him, but he seems to be feeling me a lot more."

"Sit down."

She and I sat on a barstool, and Isaiah joined us. I grabbed her hand and lowered my head. "Listen. You're not as sensitive and emotional as most women. It's no one's fault. You grew up in a house full of boys, and you were raised by your father. There were no women around for you to really look up to. I'm literally surprised you ended up in a heterosexual relationship."

She gave me the side-eye like that scenario was farfetched. She grew up playing football in the backyard with me and the boys, and I even caught her looking at nudes of women on Isaiah's phone. She was only nine, and he was almost nineteen. I'd caught her watching porn as well. It was always women on women. So when she had a boyfriend in college and started wearing heels and dresses, I was beyond shocked.

All her life, I'd bought dresses that she'd refused to wear. When I started thinking about what could have changed that when she started college, I quickly put it out of my mind. Thinking about my baby being turned out by some punk was the last thing I wanted to think about. That was the only thing I thought could have changed her though.

"So you're saying that I'm more like a man and not as soft as a woman?"

"I'm saying that you aren't the typical woman in that aspect. There's nothing wrong with that. You're not more like a man, baby. You're just different. Is he complaining about that?"

"No. I just feel weird that I'm never the one to really initiate contact. I don't communicate my feelings as much. He has to question me a lot about how I feel, and it makes me feel inadequate."

"Never feel inadequate, sis. You are who you are. If there is something you don't like about yourself, work on changing it if possible. If it's not possible, then work on loving yourself for the way you are. I don't mind helping you with that. You know that," Isaiah added.

Alexz stood from her seat and walked over to Isaiah and hugged him. "This is why you're my favorite. Everybody else brushes me off, especially Chad's punk ass."

I rolled my eyes, because without turning around, I knew Chad was joining us in the kitchen just by how she said that. I stood from my seat, and she came to me and hugged me as Chad said, "I got'cho punk ass."

When she stepped away from me, he picked her up, as she screamed, and ran around the house with her. *Lord, have mercy.* They kept me young.

***

I hope you're having a great day. I could barely concentrate on the service.

I felt warm inside when I read Anissa's text message. We'd eaten our meal and were watching a basketball playoff game. Glancing around the room to see no one was really paying attention to me, I switched my phone to vibrate and messaged her back.

I'm having a good day. It would progress to being a great day if I could see you again.

I smiled slightly when I noticed the bubbles show up on the screen, indicating she was responding. I brought my attention to the game as I waited. Chad yelled at the TV when Curry hit the three, and everybody else was on their feet cheering. Watching and playing sports was one thing that we frequently did together. I didn't play as much as I did when they were younger, but every now and then, they talked me into it when none of their friends showed up.

When my phone vibrated, I brought my attention to it. It was a message from Anissa. *That can be arranged.* There was a blushing smiley face afterward. *Jamel isn't in town this weekend, and DJ usually leaves around five.*

I smiled. Before I could respond, I realized how quiet it had gotten. I looked up and saw Shyrón frowning. He'd gotten here late and didn't know about last night. Neither did Alexz. "What's got you smiling like that?" he asked.

He could be just as blunt as Chad. He was practically Chad's shadow growing up, wanting to do everything Chad did. Now, he was putting that bluntness to use in the courtroom as an attorney. His mind was sharp when it came to the law, but the nigga acted like he didn't have much common sense, especially regarding women. He was somewhat arrogant and could be downright rude. Between him and Chad, I often wondered who raised them, because it couldn't have been me.

"I went out last night, Shy. You and Alexz were late to the party, so you missed the conversation."

Alexz frowned. "With a woman? Who?"

"Dexter's mother, Anissa."

Alexz's face brightened. "Oh, Daddy, she's so beautiful. I couldn't help but admire her from afar yesterday. She seems really nice too."

I nodded in agreement. "She is."

"She was so nice he didn't wanna come home. He just got here right before eleven."

I rolled my eyes, but I wasn't surprised that Chad would finish telling my business. Shyrón nodded repeatedly with a smile on his face. I slowly shook my head. "It wasn't like that. Chad, if you gon' tell my business, tell the whole story. Asshole. I stayed the night, but nothing happened. We just clicked, and we enjoyed one another's company."

They didn't need to hear all the stuff I told Isaiah. He was the only one who could handle that seriously. As I talked, I noticed he wasn't paying us the least bit of attention. He was still watching the game. Going back to my phone, I quickly answered Anissa's text. *I'll call you as soon as my bunch leaves to see if we can set something up.*

"Well, I'm happy for you. I'm sure we can all agree that we've wanted this for Dad for a long time," Alexz said. "You've sacrificed for us, and now it's past time that you did what makes you happy."

She flopped on the couch next to me and kissed my cheek, then suffered a thrown pillow to the face. She lunged at Chad, and I lowered my gaze back to my phone to see Anissa had messaged back. *Perfect. I can't wait.*

I smiled again. I couldn't wait either. As soon as this game was over, I would kick these Bébé's kids right out the door.

7

Anissa

IT WAS A SHAME THE WAY I KEPT ZONING OUT DURING CHURCH. All I could think about was how good I felt in Sheldon's arms. I'd slept so soundly. I could only hope that he was able to rest as well as I had. Waking up to him was so surreal. It had been years since I'd experienced that without fear that I was too softhearted or open. The couple of times that Dexter had gotten clean and I'd opened my heart up to him again, it wasn't long before I regretted it.

No matter what happened between Sheldon and I or what this led to, I was grateful it seemed to be helping both of us. Dexter had come over after church and inquired about my date. I decided to tell him that Sheldon stayed overnight. I was more than sure that if I didn't tell him, he would find out. He was about to have an entire fit, thinking that he'd taken advantage of me, until I gave him details of what happened.

He calmed down and fussed about me purposely leaving out the details so he could have a heart attack. I couldn't help but laugh at him. When I let him know that he was coming over again, he respected my privacy and left early. Maybe he could move on with his life now, since he knew I was okay. Jamel would be in town next weekend, so I knew this time was perfect for us to continue getting to know one another. I would love to introduce them next weekend if things continued going the way they did last night.

When the doorbell rang, I looked around my apartment then made my way to the door. I was a clean person, but I wanted to be sure that nothing was out of place. Taking a nervous but excited breath in, I opened the door. I smiled brightly then greeted him. "Hi, Sheldon. Come on in."

He smiled back, and that made me feel great. Just from being around him yesterday evening and last night, I quickly learned he wasn't a smiler. Once he came inside, he responded, "Hey, Anissa."

The moment I closed the door and turned to him, he pulled me into his arms. I involuntarily let out a soft moan in his embrace. It just felt good. "Come have a seat. I turned on the basketball game. I'm a Laker's girl, but I'll watch just about anybody play."

He slightly rolled his eyes. "Please tell me you aren't a band-wagoner."

"Uh... no, sir. I've been a fan since my dad introduced me to them back in the late seventies. They've been my team since then. I saw Magic come and go. Don't do me."

He chuckled as he sat and pulled me in his arms. When he kissed the side of my head, I turned toward him and smiled then kissed his soft lips. He stared into my eyes for a moment, then said, "I guess I'll let'chu make it then."

"Mmm. You guess, huh?"

"Yeah," he said as his face got closer to mine.

I thought he would kiss me again, but instead, he journeyed to the side of my head as he held me close. "You smell so good, Anissa."

"You do too."

My insides shuddered as he kissed my ear. I brought my hand to his neck and slid it up the back of his head as my eyes closed. Nothing about the feeling felt rushed or uncomfortable. I just needed him close, and I didn't even understand why. His presence seemed to be everything I needed. His hand slid up my thigh, and the shiver that went up my spine caused me to release a soft moan. Sheldon slowly pulled away from me, sliding his face against mine. *Jesus Christ of latter-day saints!*

The moment his eyes met mine, his lips met mine too. The kiss was even more passionate than the ones we shared last night, and when his tongue slid inside my mouth, I was so ready for it. It didn't last long though. *Definitely not long enough.* When he pulled away, he said, "I'm sorry. I've been thinking about you all day. Now that I'm with you, I got a little carried away."

"I've been thinking about you too. Feel free to get carried away any time you want."

I knew that I was giving him permission to take things further, and I had to wonder if I was truly ready to go all the way with another man. My body surely craved him, but I didn't want to beat myself up afterward. He stared at me then nodded. He put his arm around me and turned to the TV. "I'll make a mental note of that. I don't want you to think that that's all I want. What do you like to do outside of being home?"

I chuckled. I'd made it clear last night that I enjoyed my alone time. Turning to him slightly, I said, "I enjoy spending time with my family, skating, going to the movies, and traveling. Traveling is a new thing. I could never really afford to travel before I sold my house."

"Skating? I haven't skated in years. I would surely bust my ass if I tried now."

"Maybe, maybe not. Only one way to find out."

"That's true."

"What all do you like to do besides watch basketball?"

"I enjoy making things with my hands. I did my backyard myself.

I enjoy spending time with my family... and you," he said as he slid his fingertips down my cheek then to the hair on my shoulder.

"I hope you continue to enjoy spending time with me. I enjoy spending time with you too. It might become an obsession."

"That's a good thing, Anissa."

The way he said my name was going to drive me insane and have me doing all kinds of crazy things. My middle was pulsating. It was hard enough resisting him last night with his stiffness against me. He wanted me, and I wanted him. *What were we waiting for?* We were both over the age of fifty... too old to not know what we wanted. Looking up at him, I lifted my hand and slid my fingers through his beard then gently pulled him to me. "I really enjoy kissing you."

"Is that right?" he probed in a low voice against my lips. "I'm trying to be a gentleman, Anissa, but you're pushing me into dangerous territory."

"But what if I'm the one that's in danger? You won't venture out to rescue me?"

He licked his lips then slid his hand over my shoulder, taking my oversized shirt with it, then kissed my shoulder. "If you're in danger, then I'm coming. No doubt, baby."

He slid my bra strap off my shoulder as I shivered. Feeling his lips on my skin was driving me crazy. It felt like I was being teased, but I decided to let him lead. I was ready... beyond ready, but I wasn't so sure about just how comfortable he was with this. As he littered my shoulder and neck with kisses and strokes of his tongue, I held his head in my hands, gently pulling his ears. When he groaned into my neck then gently bit my earlobe, I moaned in response.

Sliding his arm under me, he stood from the couch and scooped me up, heading to my bedroom. God... him holding me in his arms this way was about to have me orgasming on myself. When he lowered me to the bed, he stared at me for a moment. I couldn't help but notice the bulge in his pants, and I prayed that I would be able to handle it, being that it had been so long.

However, before he could take off the first article of clothing, my phone started ringing, and the doorbell was ringing like crazy. I frowned then stood and kissed his lips. "Give me a minute."

I grabbed my phone first, because I was scared as hell to open that door. The first person I thought about was Dexter. *Had he found me?* The call was coming from DJ, so I answered. "Hello?"

"Come to the door, Ma. It's an emergency."

Sheldon was standing right next to me by the time I ended the call. "Everything okay?"

"I don't know."

I rushed to the door and opened it for DJ. "Sorry for interrupting your time with Mr. Berotte, but Jamel was in a car wreck. We need to get to Houston."

I glanced back at Sheldon to see him grabbing his keys. I nodded, feeling completely emotional. I hurriedly went to get my purse and keys then hugged Sheldon. "I'll call you."

"Okay. Be careful."

He and DJ shook hands as I locked the door then followed my son to his car. Maybe this was a sign. It wasn't time to share my goodies with the first man since Dexter that had me all in my feelings.

***

I WAS STANDING IN THE ER A TOTAL MESS AND IN TOTAL SHOCK. Jamel had been in an accident. He was only being scanned for broken bones and having an MRI done. He was in pain, but there didn't seem to be any serious injuries. The part that was shocking was that Dexter Senior was in the waiting room with us, and he looked clean. I'd been standing here for what felt like nearly five minutes, just staring at him. DJ grabbed my hand and said, "Come have a seat, Ma."

I willingly let him lead me to a seat as my phone vibrated. I knew it was probably Sheldon, and to get my mind off Dexter, I answered. "Hello?"

My voice sounded weak, and suddenly, I wished I was back in his arms. "Hey, Nissa. Have y'all made it there?"

"Yes. We got here about five or ten minutes ago, and the moment we walked in, the doctor was looking for us to tell us that Jamel didn't have any noticeable serious injuries and that they still had X-rays and an MRI to run to be sure."

"That's good news, right? Why do you sound so upset?"

"It is good news. I guess I just got too worked up wondering if he was okay." I took a deep breath. "Thank you, Sheldon."

"No thanks needed. I just wanted to check on you. Call me when you can."

"Okay. Bye."

When I ended the call, I looked over to DJ. He didn't seem the least bit surprised to see his father, and he greeted him like they'd been in touch. "You knew he would be here, didn't you?"

"I had a feeling he would be. He's been living with Jamel."

My eyes widened. How dare they keep that from me? "That's why Jamel always insisted that he came to Beaumont to visit. He didn't want me to visit him, because he had Dexter living with him," I said more to myself than to DJ.

"Mama, we—"

I held my hand up. I didn't want an explanation. They'd kept that from me. DJ knew how tormented I was for months because I didn't know if Dexter was okay or not. "Why did y'all leave me in the dark?"

"We wanted you to move on with your life and to quit worrying about Dad. After that last incident and you had gotten moved, Jamel ran into him when he'd come to visit. Told him he had one time to screw him over. They've been together ever since... nearly a year ago."

I glanced over at him to see him watching us. I could see in his eyes that he wanted to approach us. "Why would you let me be blindsided by this, DJ? Why not at least tell me on the way here?"

"I don't know, Ma. It was the wrong decision, and I apologize."

I stood from my seat and headed to the exit. I needed some air. Going to the bench right outside the door, I took a seat and stared out at the parking lot, wondering why it even mattered. The boys stepped up for their father when I could no longer handle it. They did right by him. Maybe I wasn't firm enough with him. While this should have been a great moment, it somehow turned into a moment of self-bashing. In seconds, I'd convinced myself that I wasn't good enough. Lowering my head to my hands, I let out a few tears. "Anissa?"

The sound of his voice caused a shiver to course through me. Not the same shiver I felt with Sheldon though. This shiver was one of fear and coldness. That let me know what I felt for Sheldon was genuine, although I never doubted that fact. Lifting my head, I stared up at Dexter. He gave me a soft smile while I maintained my serious expression. I didn't trust him.

"Can I sit?"

I stood from my seat and said, "Have at it."

I sacrificed everything, and I could see that in this moment, he was still expecting me to sacrifice. As I paced, I contemplated calling Sheldon to come get me. I needed to see my son though. I had to lay my eyes on him and be sure that he was okay. The doctor's word wasn't enough for me. When I turned back to Dexter, he was still standing. "There's enough room for the both of us, Anissa."

"No, there isn't. There hasn't been enough room for the both of us for years. It has been all about you for the past seventeen years, Dexter, two years before I'd had enough. This past year, I made a promise to myself... that I would put myself first. I feel like you're here to tear all of that down."

"No. That's not why I'm here. I haven't been allowed to reach out to you for obvious reasons. The boys told me that was a stipulation to their help. They wouldn't even talk about you to me. I realized then that our ship had sailed on without me. Whether I wanted to accept it or not, you were moving on. We've been divorced for a long time, but you were holding on, hoping that I would finally get myself together."

He stepped closer to me as I backpedaled. He held his hands up in a surrendering manner. "I'm sorry, Anissa. That's all I wanted to say. I'm sorry for all the years you sacrificed your happiness for me. I love you, and I will always love you. I'm not proud of the person I became after Mama died. I hurt you and our kids and refused to accept responsibility for that. Truth is, I didn't know how to. I didn't know how to go on without the woman that gave so much of herself to make sure I always had what I wanted and needed. I didn't realize at the time that the woman I was with was doing the same thing for me, and my actions were slowly destroying her."

I was standing there speechless as I stared at him. He'd rendered me that way with his words, accepting accountability for the mess he'd put us in. Turning away, I swallowed hard. I often wondered what our lives would have been like had he not gotten on drugs... where our marriage would be now that the boys were grown men. I walked back to the bench and flopped on it, continuing to stare out at the parking lot.

Dexter eased down next to me and stared out at the lot as well. Finally, he said, "Please forgive me."

"I forgave you a long time ago. It's how I was able to finally move on. I forgave you, and I forgave myself. For a while, I felt guilty for giving up on you. It wasn't until I came to the conclusion that you'd given up on yourself long before I did, that I was truly able to let go and move on. There was no way I could help you if you didn't want to help yourself. I'm glad the boys were able to help. However, that makes me feel like shit as your wife... ex-wife. To know that I wasn't enough for you was hurtful."

"You were more than enough. Seeing how much I hurt you was killing me. The last time I came to your house, I'd made up in my mind that I wanted and needed help. When I saw the for-sale sign and that the house was empty, I sat on the porch and cried until the police made me leave. I took too long to get fed up with the way I was living. I don't know how you put up with my addiction for fourteen years. I've been clean for a little over a year, thanks to DJ and Jamel."

He slid his hand to mine, and I jumped. I didn't want him touching me. While my anger had subsided, I didn't want to be reminded of his touch. The only touch I wanted was Sheldon's. Standing from my seat again, I paced in front of him. "I'm sorry, Anissa."

I glanced at him but kept pacing as I noticed DJ watching us. This was some bull, and I wasn't prepared to deal with this. Everything in me was wanting to get away from him. I left him sitting there and headed back inside and went to the coffee pot. I needed some liquor to spike this with. My nerves were so heightened they were high-fiving Jesus. When I turned back around, I saw DJ sitting next to Dexter, and I could only pray that since my nerves were in Jesus's hands that He would keep me near the cross.

8

Sheldon

It had been a long ass night. My dick had been throbbing since I'd left Anissa's house, and even after jacking off, that shit wouldn't calm down. I'd gotten so worked up. That wasn't supposed to happen, and that was probably why something happened to prevent it. I'd been thinking about the tight, warm embrace my shit would have been in since I left though. I hated what happened to her son, but shit!

When I got home, I'd come to my bedroom and just stared at Marie's picture on my nightstand. I was letting go, and while it felt good earlier, it pained me something fierce now. My heart was in a sunken place, and I didn't know what to do to bring it out other than to leave the house. It was nearly midnight, and normally, I would be asleep by now. I'd had a drink and tossed and turned for the past two hours.

I hadn't heard back from Anissa, and I was thinking that was probably what was best. *Who in the hell did I think I was?* Marie was the woman I was supposed to live my life with. Just because she was taken away from me prematurely didn't mean there was another woman out there for me. Anissa was a beautiful and sweet woman, but I belonged to Marie.

I stood from the bed and changed into my workout clothes to head to the gym. It was the best way to sort out my thoughts and emotions. Instead of continuing to mourn Marie's absence, I needed to start celebrating the life she lived. It seemed I was almost obsessed though. There had to be some middle ground. I just couldn't find it.

When I got to World Gym, I saw Dylan's car and immediately regretted coming. He was a personal trainer in his spare time and had been begging me to become one of his clients. Most likely, if he was here at this time of night, it was because he had a client. He wouldn't have time to give me, which would be fine by me.

Pulling my hood over my head, I walked inside to see he was lifting weights. He noticed me immediately. *Shit!* He frowned and made his way to me as I went to the elliptical. "Why you tryna act like you didn't see me? What'chu doin' up in here this late?"

I glanced over at him but refused to answer his questions. When I got the settings how I liked them, I began my workout, but he canceled my shit. I huffed then looked over at him. He didn't say a word... just stared at me, waiting on answers to his questions.

"I don't feel like talking, Dylan. I'm here because I couldn't sleep."

"You know I don't really get in your business like that, Dad, but maybe you need to talk things through. I may not be the best person to listen, but I love you and want what's best for you. What happened? You were happy earlier today."

He started my machine and got on the one next to me as I glanced at him. I knew he was right, but I didn't want to sound vulnerable or weak. I'd always put on a strong front for them. Isaiah was the only one to see me that way. Dylan was my baby boy... damn near my twin. I was the only parent he remembered. I had a special bond with all my kids. Our bond was that we understood one another. I didn't push him to talk about shit, and normally, he didn't push me. We respected one another's boundaries and space. Not so today.

"I went to meet Anissa. We were having a good time talking, and things started to get heated. Just as we were about to..." I paused as I glanced over at him.

I wasn't used to speaking to him this way, and I was uncomfortable as hell. Sure, we'd talked about sex, but I never had a sex life to talk about. Being that I never really discussed my personal life and decisions with him was what made this moment uncomfortable. My vulnerabilities were usually reserved for Isaiah and now... Anissa.

"Dad, I'm twenty-five years old. Something is wrong if I can't handle this conversation. I'm sure I've experienced more sexual shit than you could even think about," he said with a straight face.

I rolled my eyes slightly and continued. "We both wanted it. It's the horniest I've been since losing your mother. Just as we were about to get undressed, DJ showed up. Her youngest son had gotten in a car wreck in Houston. She had to leave."

"That's fucked up. Hopefully, he's okay, and y'all can pick up where you left off."

"That's the problem. I don't think I want to. I feel guilty as hell... like this wasn't meant to be. We weren't supposed to experience what we were embarking on."

"You think too much. Shit happens. Maybe the timing was off. That doesn't mean you aren't supposed to experience her in that manner. I'm sure that Mom was an amazing woman. Isaiah and Chad used to tell us stories of just how in love y'all were and how playful you were. After nearly twenty-five years, another woman has come along that makes you feel again. That has to be right, Dad. It has to be. Don't let your future walk away because you're holding on to the past."

I was stunned into silence because I wasn't expecting such sound advice from my baby boy. Maybe Isaiah or even Shyrón, but not him and definitely not Chad. I could only nod as the sweat dripped down my face. We remained silent for a bit as we worked out. I couldn't help but think about what he said. It wasn't something I hadn't heard before, but I suppose it was something I needed to hear right now.

After working on the machine for thirty minutes, I got off, and he did as well. I wiped my face with napkins provided in the corner of the room then turned to Dylan. "What are you doing here this late?"

"I had a client at eleven and decided to get a workout in. I'm having some issues as well. This woman that I've been messing around with is pregnant. She's married, and I always strap up, but I'm worried. She says it's for her husband, but my mind is fucked up. It's like this is my wakeup call. You probably already know, but I fuck around quite a bit without a care. It's crazy as hell. I know you didn't raise us that way, but for some reason, it didn't bother me to be with multiple women."

"Son, it's human nature. It takes effort to commit to one woman. Monogamy isn't easy. That's why so many people fail at it. However, when you meet the right one, you won't even miss the freedom to hit it and quit it. She'll be everything you're subconsciously craving. You are almost an exact replica of me. I was the same way before meeting your mother. Although I was younger than you, I was fucking just to say that I was," I said, choosing to be open with him.

He really seemed to be struggling with what he was dealing with. I could see the turmoil in his eyes when he spoke about it. "As far as you fucking with a married woman, that's off-limits, son. I don't care how unhappy she claims to be. That shit is dangerous as hell. What if the baby isn't for her husband and he comes looking for you? It's one thing to fuck around, but with married women? Naw. That ain't cool."

He rubbed the top of his head and hung it in defeat. I put my arm around him. "What you ain't gon' do, though, is stress over it. If it's your baby, you gon' do what you have to do to take care of it. However, as of right now, you can start making changes. As recent as it may be, that shit is in the past. There's nothing you can do about it now. All you can do is learn from it, move on, and try to be the best version of yourself you can be."

And just like that, my problems were no longer on my mind. It was all about Dylan and his dilemma. It had been that way for the past twenty-five years. I would find something else to concentrate on and push my issues to the back of my mind... not properly dealing with them.

"Thanks, Dad. I fucked up for real, but I definitely have to move on. So, if I have to move on, so do you. Tomorrow, call Ms. Anissa. I'm sure she could use the support, especially if y'all are as involved as I think y'all are. Deal?"

I took a deep breath and stared at him for a second then smiled and shook his hand. "Deal."

<hr />

I LIED TO MY SON. I DIDN'T CALL ANISSA. IT HAD BEEN THREE days, and I had chosen to give her radio silence. The uneasy part about that was that she was giving me the same. She hadn't called or texted me since we last talked when she found out that her son would be okay. I didn't know if she was having doubts about what was happening between us or what. It wasn't easy to forget about her though. However, being that it was the last week of school, I had shit to do to keep me occupied.

I'd been volunteering as I normally did. While the kids were in class were the toughest times. I literally had nothing to do. Being that I wasn't the friendliest person, no one really talked to me. They'd become acquainted with my persona since the beginning of the school year. So now that I needed the distraction of meaningless conversation, I couldn't get it.

As I waited for the last class to be dismissed, I decided to check on my kids. It seemed they all had their own shit going on, and the last thing I wanted to do was burden them with my ongoing issues of letting go of a woman that had involuntarily let go of me over two decades ago. I started at the top and made my way down.

To Isaiah: *What's up, Zay? How's everything going with that case? Have you made any progress?*

Second born: *What's up, ignant nigga? I hope your day is going well.*

That message was to Chad. I had him saved in my phone as second born. This was how I greeted him every time I texted him. He was about the only one that I was still somewhat playful with. Moving down the list, I sent Shyrón the next message. *Hey, son. Just checking in. Hope your day is going well.*

How's everything going, Dylan? Hope your day is going well.

To Alexz: *Hey, baby girl. I hope all is well and things are going okay with the guy you've been talking to. Hopefully I'll get to meet him soon.*

After lowering my phone to wait for their responses, I opened my bottle of Coke and took a swig. I didn't drink soda often, but today was just one of those days. My phone vibrated, so I picked it up to see who was responding, only to see a message from Anissa. I damn near started sweating immediately, wondering what she had to say. I took a deep breath then opened it.

Hello, Sheldon. I wanted to apologize for not reaching out for the past three days, but I've been dealing with some really stressful issues. I'm somewhat disappointed that you haven't reached out to me, not knowing if my son could have taken a turn for the worse or not. I'm not sure if you are going through some things or not, so I won't hold it against you. I do miss you. I just wanted to be in the right headspace whenever I reached out.

My heart sank. I felt like shit for not reaching out now. Before I could respond, the bell rang. I quickly responded. *I'm sorry. I'll text you as soon as I leave the school.*

I quickly stood to watch these bad ass kids, to make sure they got their asses out of the school without fighting, so I could go home. I didn't know what I would say to Anissa, nor did I know how to even explain my thought process, because I barely understood the shit myself. I could feel my phone vibrate a few times as I walked the halls. I knew it was probably my crew all texting back. I knew they were all still at work when I messaged, but I tended to do that at least once a week. If I didn't, they thought something was wrong.

I didn't know what I would do once summertime came. I wouldn't have anything to do to keep me busy. *If you established something with Anissa, you would have plenty to do.* I frowned slightly because I didn't know where the thought even came from. My mind was so fucking conflicted I didn't know whether I was coming or going. It was driving me crazy. When I was with her, I didn't have a single doubt about whether I should be there. It was when I was away from her that my mind worked overtime. That could possibly be a sign that I was putting myself through unnecessary shit... making myself crazy in the process.

As I watched the kids leave, I thought about what I would do when I left the school. Maybe I could go work out. *Or maybe you could go and talk to Anissa in person.* I slowly shook my head and continued walking through the halls. When I saw Dylan walking my way, I got nervous. He was a P.E. coach at an elementary school here in Beaumont, but he never came to the high schools.

"Hey, son. What are you doing here?"

"Hey. Just thought we could spend some time together. You feel like shooting pool and going to dinner?"

"Yeah. Sure. How was work?"

Since our talk the other day, he'd been really gravitating toward me. We'd talked every day, either by text or phone call. Now, today, he wanted to spend time with me. In years past, I was the last one he wanted to kick it with. Not that we didn't get along, because I got along with all my kids. He just seemed to shy away from me. He would much rather hang out with his friends or his brothers. However, I wasn't at all disappointed by him reaching out more.

I watched the girls pass us and stare at him too long. These lil fast ass girls got on my nerves. When I first started volunteering, they had the nerve to flirt with me until I cursed them out. My exact words would be, *I don't work for the school. I can tell you exactly what I wanna tell you. Get the fuck to class.*

They would pretend to be so offended, but then the next day, they would still be staring at me with googly eyes. I glanced down to see that Dylan was wearing black wind pants. *Long as he wasn't wearing those damn gray sweatpants.* He slowly shook his head. "These lil girls a trip. I like grown women."

"That's good to know. I'd beat the fuck out your ass myself if I ever found out you were messing with one of these lil girls."

He chuckled and shook his head. "Well... the woman that's pregnant is a teacher. She works at the school with me."

"That's some messy shit, boy."

He slid his hand down the top of his head and said, "Yeah, I know. I couldn't say no when she approached me. She so damn fine. This situation done changed me forever though."

"That's all that matters. Let's get out of here. Although this place gives me something to do, I can't wait until school is out."

He chuckled. "You would have something to do had you kept your word and messaged Ms. Anissa."

I slightly rolled my eyes as we walked out of the doors. "She messaged me, so I have to call when we leave. I'll follow you."

He gave me a smirk and said, "A'ight."

We went our separate ways, and when I got in my car, I grabbed my phone. Before I lost the nerve, I called her. Hopefully she wasn't busy or somewhere that she couldn't answer. It rang three times, and just as I was about to end the call, she answered. "Hello?"

She sounded out of breath like she was running or something, so I said, "Hey, Anissa. Is this a bad time?"

"No. I just got off the treadmill. How have you been?"

"I'm okay... struggling a bit. How's your son?"

"He's fine. He went home today. What are you struggling with? I mean... I think I know, but I want to hear it from you."

"My conscience has been beating me up, and my mind has been

driving me crazy. It's like... all I can think about is you, but my conscience is making me feel guilty about it."

"Did you ever call a grief counselor?"

"No."

"I have the number to a good one if you want it."

"Yeah. Are you back in town?"

"I came back Monday night. I uhh... I needed to get away from there. My ex-husband showed up. He's clean and has been living with my son for the past year. They kept that from me. So when I showed up at the hospital and he was there, it knocked me off my square. I'm thinking about taking a trip next week, just to reset."

I sat there thinking about asking to go with her until Dylan blew his horn at me. I backed out of my parking spot and followed behind him while remaining silent, trying to filter through my thoughts. There was no reason why I couldn't go. Breaking my silence, I asked, "Where are you going?"

"Probably New Orleans. I can have some fun while I'm there, and it's not too far away in case I need to get back here quickly for whatever reason. Why do you ask?"

I wanted to close my eyes and pray about what I was about to say, but I didn't have that luxury since I was driving. "Can I go with you?" I blurted.

The line went completely quiet. After a few seconds, she asked, "Do you think that would be a good idea? I mean... there's no telling what could happen between us. Once we go all the way, I will be extremely offended if you ghosted me, Sheldon. I'm really feeling you, and I'm sure about how I feel and what I want, despite my past showing up and throwing me for a loop. I like you, but I'd rather know now if I'm just spinning my wheels."

As I turned in the parking lot of the pool hall, I thought about what she said. She could be right, but what if she was wrong? "Can we play it by ear this week? I'm feeling you too. When I'm around you, nothing else matters. I crave you. I just don't know how to make the thoughts stop. I understand where you're coming from though. Can I see you later?"

"Maybe. I'm going to dinner with a friend. I'll let you know."

"Okay. Well, I have to go," I said as I turned off my engine. "I'm spending time with one of my sons. I'll text you later."

"Okay."

She ended the call, and I could feel that she was trying to pull away from me. She was guarding her heart, and I couldn't blame her for that. I wasn't emotionally stable. I would do whatever I had to do, though, to assure I didn't end up living the rest of my life without her.

9

A nissa

"Yolanda, I just don't know. I was stunned. I'm not angry that they helped their dad get clean... not in the least bit. I was angry that they kept it from me and allowed me to find out the way I did."

"That's understandable."

She remained quiet for a moment while I sipped my drink. We were at Cheddar's having dinner and talking about the foolery I endured Sunday and Monday. I saw her at the gym earlier, and we decided to get dinner together since we hadn't done that in a while. Plus, we'd never gotten to celebrate my retirement. My feelings had still been on my sleeve, and I knew I just needed to talk to someone who wasn't connected to it, to be a sounding board.

I had to admit that when I saw Dexter, he practically took my breath away. He looked like the man I married... the man I loved with all of me. I should have been prepared though. The shit I went through with him... the heartache of watching him deteriorate... the sleepless nights... all of it came flooding back. Although he'd barely said a word to me Monday, just him being in my space was more than enough. My heart was so heavy until I'd begun using language that I had gotten away from using.

I rarely cursed anymore, because I always associated it with being angry or disgusted. I wanted to keep my spirit light. While I was going through it with him, I was a sailor whose mouth was on steroids. Every other word that came out of me was foul, not to mention the negativity I spewed. I was full of toxicity. While I thought love was what fueled me, the toxicity was killing me. Being around Dexter, no matter how great he looked, wasn't good for my spirit.

I'd told Yolanda all my business, and I felt better once I got it all out. She'd been a good friend to me, and she didn't try to smother me. I loved that about her. I needed my space, and so did she. She was a single woman with one son who was in college. He was only nineteen.

"So when do you leave for New Orleans?"

"Probably Monday. I don't want to pay those higher hotel fees on the weekends."

"I feel you on that. I can't wait until I'm done with this damn job so I can just take off like that."

Just as I was about to respond to her, it felt like someone was staring at me. When I looked up and saw Sheldon, I almost pissed on myself. He looked so good. He wore a beige t-shirt that read *Daddy*, and Lord have mercy did he embody that word in every way. "Who is that?" Yolanda asked.

When I looked back at her, I noticed the smirk on her face. "He's uhh... DJ's friend's dad. I went to a barbeque at his house Saturday with him."

"Mm hmm."

I ignored her and drank more of my drink, doing my best to ignore Sheldon. He was here with one of his sons. He hadn't seen me, and I wanted to keep it that way. He'd given me a lot to think about on our phone conversation earlier. Interacting with him would only cloud my judgment. Just as I was looking away from him, I met eyes with the culprit that had been staring at me since we'd gotten here. He winked then blew me a kiss. I frowned in disgust as I turned away. Thankfully, Sheldon and his son weren't seated close to us. However, if he scanned the area, he would see me on the other side of the room. As the waitress arrived with our food, I couldn't be more grateful. My stomach was on E, coasting on fumes.

She set our food in front of us, and I sniffed my alfredo as I closed my eyes. When I opened them, Yolanda was laughing, and she was saying something, but I couldn't hear a thing. My eyes had met Sheldon's, and I had suddenly gone deaf. The moment he stood from his seat, I got hot like the flames of hell were burning in my soul. I was so disappointed when he didn't call to check on me in those three days. It made me feel like he was playing games. I didn't want to take a risk on a man that wasn't willing to take a risk on me.

When he got to our table, he gave me a slight smile and said, "Hi, Anissa."

"Hey."

I stood from my seat so it wouldn't seem awkward, and he pulled me into his arms. When I heard his exhale, it caused me to close my eyes and relax in his embrace. It was like no one else was there for a moment. After pulling away from me, he stared into my eyes then glanced at Yolanda. "This is my friend, Yolanda. Yolanda, this is Sheldon."

He nodded at her, and she did the same then resumed eating. "It's good to see you," he said as he grabbed my hand.

"It's good to see you too."

"Okay. I'll let you get back to your food before it gets cold. Talk to you later?"

"Yeah. Okay."

He kissed my cheek then turned and walked away. I stood there for a moment before I could sit down. There was no question on whether I would see him later. It was inevitable, which was why I was trying to fly under the radar. After feeling the intensity in that encounter, I knew that seeing him would always be on a need-to basis.

I sat on my couch, nervously awaiting Sheldon's arrival. I'd messaged him, letting him know that I was home. He immediately called to see if he could come over. Crossing my legs, I did my best to remain calm. Watching my wine swirl around my glass as I nervously rotated it, I couldn't help but wonder where today's visit would lead. Neither of us were in the frame of mind we were in before Jamel's accident.

I hoped that he was coming to talk about what happened between us and what thoughts led to his radio silence. One would think that after nearly twenty-five years, he would have moved on by now. It wasn't like she was popping in and out of his life like Dexter was doing to me. This couldn't be healthy. He was still feeling guilty about being with me as if he were cheating on his wife.

Standing from the couch, I made my way to the kitchen, gulping the wine while en route. That wine wasn't helping a thing. I took a bottle of cognac from the cabinet and poured myself a little then started my smooth jazz playlist on my phone. After taking a sip, I stared at the glass while it went down, then ended up gulping it like I'd done the wine and nearly choked myself to death. I was not about that life. *Who am I trying to fool?*

I went to the fridge and grabbed a bottle of water to calm my throat down. As soon as I put the top back on the bottle, the doorbell rang. I was so nervous jitters had taken control of my body. Once I checked the peephole and saw just how fine Sheldon looked in his sweats and t-shirt, I took a deep breath and thought, *Here goes nothing*. Grabbing the doorknob, I turned it slowly, silently questioning if

I was doing the right thing by allowing him a chance to ghost me all over again.

Giving in to my heart, I pulled the door open and stepped aside as I said, "Hey. Come in."

He gave me a tight-lipped smile then walked in and waited for me to close the door. When I turned around, he grabbed me by the hand and led me to my couch. "Would you like a drink before I have a seat?"

"No. I think I've had enough to drink today."

I smiled then sat next to him. I angled my body slightly as I leaned against the cushions. He seemed a little nervous, so I decided to steer the conversation in a different direction. "Which son was that with you today?"

He smiled and seemed to relax instantly. "That was Dylan. He's the baby boy."

"He looks the most like you."

"Yeah. He's more like the old me than I even knew. He's only a year older than my daughter."

"How's he like you?"

"He's resilient. No matter what's thrown his way, he conquers it. He's been reminding me of how much I liked the old me. This new me is miserable."

He lowered his head and twiddled his thumbs. I slid my hand over his, and he quickly grabbed it like it was his lifeline. We sat there silently in the moment as he seemed to struggle with what he wanted to say. Covering our intertwined fingers with my other hand, I did my best to console him by rubbing it slowly and gently.

Finally finding the words, I asked, "Why don't you do something about it?"

He slid his hand down his beard then turned to me. "That's why I'm here, Anissa. Those three days were hell, but for some reason, I couldn't come out of it. However, when you're communicating with me and we're around one another, I can't help but to feel like you're the missing piece in my life. Being with you is a high like no other.

The excitement of what's to come sends my adrenaline into overdrive."

He lifted his head, staring into my eyes. When I saw how glossy his had gotten, it brought tears to my eyes. I swallowed them back then responded to what he said. "Sheldon, I feel all that, too, but I think we need to take this slow. You're still grieving your wife. What will I do if I fall for you only for you to disappear on me because you feel guilty?"

"I understand. As long as you give me the chance to prove my readiness when that time comes, then I'm good. I plan to go to counseling and get myself figured out. I truly want to know you and be with you, Anissa. I just hope that you can be patient with me."

"I've been single for fifteen years, Sheldon. I doubt I will go anywhere. I'm always going to be here for you if you want to talk."

I leaned over and kissed his cheek, and before I could pull away, he softly kissed my lips. The man gave me all the feels, and I didn't know how I was going to explain to my body what my mouth had just said. She was going to want to beat the dog crap out of me. I flipped my hair over my shoulder as he scooted over, creating a little space between us.

He nodded in acceptance of what I'd said then cleared his throat. He turned back to me and smiled slightly. "So how are you really? I can imagine that being blindsided wasn't a good thing, and it was probably hurtful. Did your sons have an excuse for not telling you?"

I nodded. "It was really hurtful, and yes, they had an excuse." I was struggling with if I wanted to tell him everything, but there was no point in withholding anything from him. It wasn't like I wanted Dexter back. "I was so in shock about him being there I developed an immediate headache. He talked to me about how our sons ended up helping him get clean. When I talked to DJ about it, he apologized about keeping it from me. He said he thought it was best that way because he wasn't sure if Dexter would relapse or not. He didn't want me to become invested all over again."

"Why did he think you would?"

"I was always trying to help Dexter get clean. Even a couple of years ago, I still had a heart for him, although we'd been divorced for years. While I was trying to move on, I still hadn't fully let go. He knew the only way I would fully let go was if I was separated from Dexter. I couldn't separate if he knew where I was or vice versa. After getting through those first few months in my apartment, he knew that if he mentioned his dad, I would want to know more. So he didn't say anything and convinced Jamel not to say anything either. I wished DJ would have at least told me before I got to the hospital."

"You're a good woman. I hate that you had to go through that with your ex. You don't have to go into detail for me to imagine what that was like. I had a brother who was strung out for years. It took my mama dying for him to get on the straight and narrow. He lives in Birmingham now and is doing well as far as I know."

"That's great."

We sat quietly for a moment as I tuned into the music that was playing. "Heaven's Here" by Robert Glasper featuring Ant Clemons was playing, and the words were striking a nerve. Apparently, they were doing the same to Sheldon, because he stood and pulled me to a standing position as well. He pulled me close, holding me in his embrace, then he began swaying to the music. The lyrics said, *why am I nervous when I know how I feel about you?* I could imagine that the words were ringing true for him even more so, since he was still struggling with what he felt for me.

He lowered his head, allowing it to rest against mine, but he didn't say a word while the song played. We just continued to sway. My body became extremely relaxed, and I laid my head against his shoulder as he soothingly rubbed my back. I wanted this man so bad, and I hated that he wasn't where I was mentally. Being hurt was the last emotion I wanted to feel with him, but I knew that if I allowed him to take things too fast, that was exactly what would happen.

As if reading my thoughts, he said, "I scheduled an appointment with a grief counselor. I go tomorrow evening after school."

"That's great, Sheldon."

That came out only a step above a whisper. I was happy that he was seeking help, but I wanted to make sure he was doing this for him. "Are you doing this for you or for me?"

"Anissa... I honestly didn't realize I needed one until I started feeling things for you. Loving my wife was never a feeling I thought odd until I started feeling guilty about wanting you. I know that it's okay to still love her, but it shouldn't be to the point that it's harmful emotionally or mentally. It's been both the past few days... since meeting you. However, I refuse to let you go. I want to show you how serious I am about getting to know you and being with you. You won't regret this. I promise."

I closed my eyes. Even if nothing came of this, I could never regret meeting him. Being around him made me feel alive in places I thought had died a long time ago. I could only pray that his counseling sessions went well, because while I wouldn't regret meeting him, I didn't want to have to go back to being without him.

10

Sheldon

"When you think of Marie, how does it make you feel?"

"I feel sorrow, depression, and sadness."

"That's what we have to work on. When you think of her, I want you to get to the point where you feel love. Depression isn't healthy. After twenty-five years... depression can kill you. I'm surprised you're healthy. Has it been this way the entire time?"

"No. It only got worse when I met Anissa a week ago. I feel things for her that I've never felt for another woman other than Marie."

"Your mind is associating those feelings to Marie. We have a lot to work on, but I promise we will get there. I'm glad you contacted my office, because men tend to have a hard time asking for help. That tells me just how determined you are to be healthy and move on in your love life. Marie will always be special, and I'm going to help you to move past the grief."

"Thank you. So when should I come back?"

"If you can come next week, that'll be great."

"Okay."

I stood from my seat and headed to the front desk. For this session, I'd mainly been telling her about myself and how Marie left this world and left me in shambles. I was desperately trying to escape the chaotic state my mind had been in for the past week and a half. We'd talked a little about my kids and what I'd been doing to try to move on from the devastation her untimely death brought.

Leaving Anissa last night was hard, but I knew she wouldn't allow me to stay... not after the feelings we'd spilled all over the place. She knew just how vulnerable I was feeling, and vulnerability, in my situation, wasn't good. I would have tried to go too far and possibly ruined anything we could possibly have.

After scheduling my appointment for next Thursday, I left the office and called Alexz. She and I were supposed to be having dinner. It had been a while since we'd gone out. We usually either had lunch or dinner twice a week, but somehow, we'd fallen off. We hadn't been out since the Thursday before the barbeque. I immediately thought about Anissa. I hadn't spoken to her yet today, but I would call as soon as I ended the phone call with Alexz.

Right before it went to voicemail, she answered. "Hey, Daddy. We still on for this evening?"

"Yeah, baby. I was calling to make sure nothing had changed for you."

"No, sir. I'll see you at six at Saltgrass."

"Okay. Are we meeting, or am I picking you up?"

"I have a couple of errands to run, so I'll meet you there."

"Okay, baby girl. See you in a couple of hours."

I ended the call as I wondered about why she sounded like she was trying to rush me off the phone. There was also a nervous tremble in her voice. Alexz couldn't hide her emotions from me or her brothers, especially Chad and Isaiah. While she had her masculine qualities at times, those feminine attributes always came shining through whenever a boy was involved... a man now. I was sure we would talk about whatever was bothering her when we got to dinner.

When I got home to shower and change, I sent Anissa a text. I had to see her tonight after Alexz and I went our separate ways. *Good evening, Anissa. I hope you had a great day. I didn't want to call first in case you were busy. Give me a call whenever you have time.*

For some reason, I felt like I was walking on eggshells where she was concerned. I didn't want to push her away, but at the same time, I didn't want to be clingy. Going on this trip with her was something I wanted so badly. I felt like it would give me the reset I needed. If she allowed me to go, I would have to invite her to Sunday dinner... her and DJ. I wanted them all to know what was going on before I left.

My kids would be happy I was enjoying the company of someone other than them, so I knew that wouldn't be an issue, but I didn't want to leave them in the dark either. As I pulled clothes out of my closet, my phone chimed. Going to it, I saw it was from Anissa. I quickly opened it to read: *My day was good. I'll call you in about five minutes. I'm leaving out of the grocery store now.*

Since she would be calling soon, I went to the kitchen to get a bottle of water and chilled out until her call came through. Today's talk had me in a different frame of mind. I wasn't feeling guarded or closed off. I was sure Alexz would be able to tell. Talking about how Marie and I met had brought a smile to my face... a huge smile. However, talking about how I felt when she died had been hard. That woman was my everything, and for her to be suddenly taken away from me and her five kids was a pill I didn't want to swallow. When I tried to swallow it, it got lodged in my throat.

It seemed I had learned to deal with Marie's absence in a somewhat toxic way. Although I'd dedicated my life to raising our kids, I'd closed myself off from everyone else. I was only living inside our bubble, that I'd created, where Marie's memory was very much alive. With almost everything the kids and I did, I would bring up how much their mother would have enjoyed it or how proud she would have been.

Breaking me from my thoughts about my counseling session, my phone rang. It was Anissa. I was excited to hear her voice. "Hello?"

"Hi, Sheldon. How are you?"

"I'm okay. How are you? How was your day?"

"It was good. I'm starting to get a little bored though. There's only so much exercise a person can do in a day's time. I'm not really good with crafts and stuff like that. I watch TV until I end up dozing, and since it's just me here, I don't cook and clean every day. However, I'm sure that's a problem a lot of people wish they had compared to them going to work."

She chuckled, and it made me smile. I could hear her shuffling around. She was probably putting up her groceries. "Well, by the time you come back from New Orleans, I'll have the entire day to myself, too, since tomorrow is the last day of school. It's not like I have to really be there. I just volunteer to give me something to do."

She was quiet for a moment, and she was no longer moving around... at least as far as I could hear. After taking a deep breath, she asked, "How did your session go?"

"It was a little tough, but it was good. I'm willing to go through all of it so I can be in a better head space when you aren't near me. The problem is never when you're around; it's always after I'm alone. I'm confident that everything will go well, simply because I want them to."

"Sounds like the old Sheldon you were speaking about yesterday is making a comeback."

I chuckled slightly. "I suppose he is. I know I shouldn't say this, but it's truly how I feel." I closed my eyes and thought about it for a second, wondering why I was even sharing so much with her this soon. I continued anyway. "You and my kids give me purpose. Had it not been for them, I probably would have grieved myself to death. Now that they're grown and I'm spending more and more time alone, it felt like my reason for wanting to live was irrelevant. They didn't need me like they did when they were little. I mean, I wasn't suicidal or nothing like that, but I surely wasn't the happiest man walking this green earth."

"Hmm. I could tell. You were quite resistant when I first met you."

"And only a week later, I can't stop thinking about you."

"While I'm flattered, Sheldon, you have to find your joy. Your love for yourself is practically nonexistent."

"It's there... barely. I love myself, but I loved myself more when Marie was alive. How I felt about myself seemed to be contingent on how I made Marie feel. I know that's not healthy, but there was nothing I could do to change it. Once she was gone, that feeling transferred to my kids. Now I have no one but myself, and it's been a battle."

"Realizing that there is a problem is the first step, but doing something about it is the next step. You're making great progress. I'm happy for you."

"Thanks. Will you be available later? I'm having dinner with my daughter, so I need to shower and get ready."

"Yeah. I'll be here. Enjoy your time with your baby."

"I'm sure I will. Talk to you later, gorgeous."

After ending the call, I went to the shower, and I had to pause before I got in. A smile spread across my face. I was going to get myself together... I had to. Anissa was the woman I wanted, and I refused to let my inner turmoil keep me from her.

◈

"Daddy, this is Knowledge Rucker. Knowledge, this is my dad, Sheldon Berotte."

I frowned slightly. Knowledge couldn't be his real name. *Could it?* I hated being caught off guard, and that was just what Alexz had done to me. She was introducing me to her boyfriend, and I was stunned. That was probably what her nerves were about on the telephone. After I'd hugged her and kissed her cheek, I'd noticed him just standing there, waiting to be introduced.

I shook his hand and nodded as he said, "It's nice to finally meet you, sir. You're all Alexz talks about."

I gave him a slight smile then turned away. This was my baby girl, and I didn't want to embarrass her, but I was ready to light into his ass, asking him all sorts of questions. I wished she wouldn't have done this at a restaurant, but she was intentional about this. She did it here so her brothers wouldn't show up. However, she must've forgotten how her brothers were. I'd informed all of them that I would be with her at Saltgrass if they were looking for me.

As we waited, I turned back to him and asked, "Is Knowledge your real name?"

"Yes, sir, it is."

I nodded. At least he had sense when he talked to me. He seemed to be very respectful. I didn't accept anything less from Alexz. She was tough and didn't stand for bullshit. She was raised by a strong man and raised with four strong men. So while I was sure she could handle herself, I was still in protective mode. Glancing at him, I could tell by his tight shoulders that he was tense. "Relax, Knowledge. If my daughter thought enough of you for us to meet, then you must be pretty decent. I trust her judgment. What do you do for a living?"

I could see his shoulders relax somewhat, but not completely. There was no telling what Alexz had told him about me. "I'm a CPA."

I nodded repeatedly. "Are you from here? Do you work here?"

"I'm actually from Ohio, but I moved down to go to school. We met at a frat party at Lamar."

"You pledged?" I asked as Alexz rolled her eyes.

I knew all the questions I was asking him was getting on her nerves, but how else did she expect me to get to know him? Before he could answer my question, the hostess got our attention to lead us to a table. Once we sat and was informed that our waitress would be with us soon, he said, "I pledged Alpha Phi Alpha, but we were at a Sigma party. When she told me she was an AKA, that was it."

I gave him a slight smile as our waitress appeared, introduced herself, and took our drink orders. Alexz was quiet as hell. Once the waitress left, I asked, "You okay, baby girl? How was your day?"

"I'm okay, Daddy. It was long. The doctor's office was packed, and some of the patients were on my last damn nerve. Sorry."

I grabbed her hand and rubbed it gently as I stared at her. She wouldn't look at me, so I knew there was more going on in that head of hers. Since we had company, I wouldn't push, but the moment we were alone, I would dig all up in her shit. Knowledge leaned over and kissed her cheek then turned his attention to me.

He took a deep breath then grabbed her hand as the waitress brought our drinks to the table. It seemed he knew what was going on and was trying to soothe her as well. Maybe that was what this dinner was about. They must've had some type of announcement. Once the waitress took our orders and had left again, Alexz's face was red. They were talking amongst themselves as I was ordering my food, so something was definitely up.

I could see that this was all Knowledge. This meeting up for dinner was his idea, and Alexz was uncomfortable with it for some reason. He looked up at me and finally said, "Mr. Berotte, I'm a good man, and I want to be everything that Alexzandria Marie Berotte needs. She's hesitant because she's so independent, and she's worried about you."

He lowered his head for a moment then looked back up at me. "I was offered a job at a CPA firm in Atlanta. I want Alexz to go with me as my fiancée. I love her so much, and I know she loves me. I just need her to trust that I can take care of her too. Plus..."

Alexz nudged him under the table, and he stopped talking. She wasn't going to shut him down now. There was no way they were going to leave me hanging. Just knowing that she thought she had to stay here to be with me was enough for me to give them my blessing.

He came to me like a man and had *been* wanting to meet me. It was Alexz that was holding things up.

When no one said anything, I asked, "Plus what?"

Alexz looked up at me with tears in her eyes, and that shit put me on high alert. Whatever hurt my baby, hurt me. I grabbed her hand as I glanced at Knowledge. His gaze was trained on her as he lifted her hand and kissed it. "Daddy, I'm pregnant."

I released a sigh of relief. I thought she was about to say she was sick or something. I smiled at her. "So, you're having my first grandbaby, and you want to get married and move to Atlanta. Is that right?"

She looked away from me. "I'm having your first grandbaby. I love Knowledge, but I don't want to move."

The tears fell from her eyes, and I knew this was serious. Alexz didn't cry in front of me a lot. I probably hadn't seen her cry since she broke her leg her tenth-grade year. "Why don't you want to move, baby girl? Besides me and your brothers, what's keeping you here?"

"Aren't you and my brothers enough? Daddy, y'all are my everything. Knowledge wants me to trust him enough for me to allow him to take me away from everyone I know and love and that I know has my back no matter what. That's a lot of trust. I can't move that far away without y'all."

She turned her attention to him and said, "So, I hate to do this to you, but you're going to have to choose. I'm not leaving my family to go fourteen hours away. Had you said Houston... even Dallas, I would have thought about it, but I probably would have conceded. Knowledge, I can*not* move all the way to Atlanta. Period. So unfortunately, it's either me or that job."

She stood from her seat and walked off just as Chad was walking toward us. I knew he would be the one to pop up. She didn't say a word to him as she walked past him, probably heading to the ladies' room. He frowned, then shook my hand and asked, "Where she going?"

"The ladies' room."

He glanced over at Knowledge and extended his hand. "I'm one of Alexz's older brothers, Chad."

"Nice to meet you. I'm Knowledge."

Chad frowned then glanced at me. I slowly shook my head, trying to coax him into leaving it alone. Before he could say anything though, Knowledge said, "It's my real name. I get that everywhere I go... mainly from my people."

He rubbed his forearm with his fingertips, indicating he was talking about black people as the white waitress appeared at the table asking Chad if he'd like to order anything. Once he had, he asked, "What's up with Alexz?"

Knowledge leaned back in his chair as I said, "Knowledge wants to marry her. She would marry him if he stayed here. He was offered a job in Atlanta."

"And she ain't moving."

"You know your sister hardheaded as hell. She doesn't want to leave us. I'm thinking that it's mainly about me," I added.

Chad frowned then said, "You know she love the hell out of me. That got to be it. Let me go knock on that bathroom door."

I rolled my eyes when he got up and walked off. "Hopefully, we won't get kicked out."

Knowledge frowned slightly, but what I saw in his eyes let me know that Alexz had a protector. I could see the hood in those eyes without him saying a word. He was on guard for bullshit. I chuckled slightly then added, "Chad is the one she argues and fights with all the time."

He nodded. "Mr. Berotte, I don't know what to do. This job is paying almost thirty grand more than what I make here. They will pay for me to relocate and everything. They're going to rent a condo for me as well. I want to provide for her and my baby. If I stay here, I feel like I'll be limiting myself."

"I'll talk to her. When do you have to give them your decision?"

"I have two weeks. If I accept the job, I'll have to start work out there two weeks later... enough time to put in a two-week notice. They will put me up in a hotel until the condo is ready."

I nodded as I saw Alexz coming back with Chad on her heels. Surprisingly, they weren't arguing. "You good, baby girl? Can't have my grandchild all frustrated."

"Hol' the hell on. What grandchild?" Chad said with a deep frown on his face.

"I'm pregnant, Chad. I haven't been to the doctor yet, but I am pregnant."

For the first time in a long time, I saw him be soft with his sister. He stood and pulled her from her seat then embraced her. "Congratulations, Alex with a Z."

After Chad shook Knowledge's hand to congratulate him and he sat down next to me, I saw the sadness in my daughter's eyes. I knew I would have to do my best to convince her to just do whatever made her happy. As he wrapped his arm around her shoulder and she leaned into him, I could clearly see that she wanted to be with Knowledge.

11

Anissa

"How are you doing, baby?"

"I'm okay, Mama. I need to apologize to you again. I hate that you had to see Pop that way. Please know that you were our main concern as to why we hadn't told you."

"Jamel, I get it. I do. I was hurt and angry at first, but I was just in shock. I understand why the two of you did what you did. I'm happy that y'all were able to get him to get clean."

"It actually wasn't hard. I think he was finally at the end of his rope. Once he didn't have you to lean on, he had no choice but to get himself together."

I lowered my head as I thought about how I'd been a crutch for Dexter. Although we weren't together, he knew I loved him with everything in me, and he used that to his benefit when he was out there on the street. There were plenty of times I'd let him stay in the garage just to get out of the cold and rain or give him a plate of food so he didn't starve to death.

I took care of his basic needs, so why did he need to get clean? There was even a shower in the garage that DJ had installed so they could shower out there after working out. Since the garage was attached to the house, it was climate controlled, so it could almost function like an apartment. I slowly shook my head as I accepted the role I played in Dexter's decline to self-destruction.

I was sitting on the couch, waiting on Sheldon to pick me up for dinner since he didn't make it to me last night, when I decided to call Jamel. He said dinner with his daughter turned into dinner with all his kids, and he didn't want to come over so late. So tonight, he was taking me to the restaurant of my choice.

"So what are they saying about your arm?" I asked Jamel.

"It's okay. I just need therapy. Had I not slammed on my brakes, that guy would have hit me right in the driver door of my car. He could have killed me. Thankfully, I was completely aware of what was going on around me."

"God is good, son. I don't know how I would have handled losing you. I'm so happy it wasn't as serious as it could have been."

"I know. They need to do something about that intersection. People run that light all the time. Someone is going to get killed if something isn't done. Well, I have to go, Ma. I'll call you tomorrow. My homegirl is bringing me something to eat, and she just got here."

"Your homegirl, huh? Bye, boy."

He chuckled then said, "I love you."

"I love you more, baby."

I ended the call as I slowly shook my head. I was so glad he was doing well. Just as I was about to go to the kitchen for a pre-dinner snack, my doorbell rang. I was starving. I knew it was Sheldon since no one else visited me. However, I was in for a surprise when I looked through the peephole and saw a woman at my door. I frowned hard as I asked, "Who is it?"

"Open the door, bitch!"

I frowned even harder as I tried to figure out who in the hell this woman was. She looked fairly young, so she had to have the wrong apartment. Before I could open the door, Sheldon appeared next to her with a bouquet of flowers in his hand. I was beyond happy that he arrived when he did, just in case this woman tried to get violent.

I opened the door, and she frowned hard as hell. "I'm sorry, but do you have a roommate?"

It was my turn to frown. "No ma'am."

I invited Sheldon inside and smiled slightly as he leaned over to kiss my lips. The woman in front of me looked perplexed. She was truly confused. "Who are you looking for?"

"Nobody. It's stupid. I'm sorry for disturbing you."

She walked off, and I was standing there just as confused as she was. Suddenly, she turned back to me and asked, "Do you know someone named Yolanda?"

I frowned. Of course I knew someone named Yolanda, but it wasn't this woman's business who I knew. "No. Why?"

"Ugh! My boyfriend is cheating on me. Apparently, he just met this woman, and she gave him this address to pick her up from tomorrow. She'd sent several pictures of herself, so I knew you weren't her as soon as you opened the door."

My eyes bucked at her revelation. "That's crazy!" I yelled. Yolanda was gon' get the business from me. "However, you need to check your man. This woman may not even know you exist."

"She obviously does. Why would she give him an address she didn't live at?"

"That's a damn good question."

"Again, I'm sorry, ma'am. I didn't mean to interrupt your date."

"No problem."

I was fuming when I closed the door. Before I could fully acknowledge Sheldon, I went to my phone and called Yolanda. She was too old for this kind of foolishness. I couldn't believe she'd done something like this. While she was much younger than me, she was too old to be playing games like this. "Hello?"

"Who did you give my address to?"

"What?"

"Who in the hell did you give my address to, Yolanda? You know how I am about my peace. Some woman showed up at my door, calling me a bitch because she thought you lived here. What is your problem?"

"Oh my God. I'm so sorry, Anissa. I... uh..."

"You were being trifling, Yolanda. I don't have time for that type of drama or negativity. I don't know who you take me for, but I'm not one to cling to people who put me in harm's way. What if that woman would have shown up with a gun and shot me? Don't talk to me, don't come to my house, forget I even existed."

I ended the call as I took deep breaths. I was so damn angry I could spit nails. The moment Sheldon's arms wrapped around me from behind, all of that began melting away. He kissed my cheek and said, "Sounds like some shit you shouldn't even be involved in. Take a few deep breaths and calm down. Your face is as red as your shirt."

I closed my eyes and did just as he said while he repeatedly kissed my cheek and head. When I rested my head against his chest, he asked, "You good?"

"Yeah. Thank you. I've been friends with her for a year. This is why I normally stick to myself. I'm sorry you had to see that, but I'm also glad that you came when you did. I haven't had to fight in a long time, but I'm almost sure I would have drug her lil ass. She would have realized quickly that she wasn't 'bout that life."

His eyebrows hiked up, and I couldn't help but laugh. I'd grown up in the projects, and while I was far removed from Lincoln Terrace, I wouldn't hesitate to resort to that if I felt threatened. Sheldon finally said, "Let me find out you a gangsta."

I laughed again. "No, not even close. I grew up in the Pear Orchard in Lincoln Terrace. It's not even called that anymore, but you know it was always some ish popping off over there back in the day. It was ratchet before there was a ratchet. I'm just thankful I wasn't a product of my environment."

"Right. Well, are you ready?"

"Yes," I said as I walked away to put my flowers in water and get my purse. "Thank you so much for the flowers. I love roses."

"Well, since this was an official date, I figured I had better come correct. So where are we going?"

"How do you feel about JWilson's?" I asked.

"I've never been there. What type of food do they sell?"

"American. You can get just about anything from sea bass to fried chicken."

"Sounds like a winner. Let's head out," he said, extending his hand to me.

I smiled at him as I grabbed his hand then walked over to him and puckered my lips. The way I felt being with him was so refreshing. Although we weren't a couple, we definitely felt like one. I knew I was the only woman he was seeing and vice versa. Had it been up to him, we would be a couple by now. I just needed to make sure he was ready for that, and I wanted to believe that he was. He smiled at me then kissed my lips. He slid his fingertips down my arm, causing my lashes to flutter. "We better go," I said softly.

"Mm hmm," he said with a slight smile.

After locking the door, I turned to him and said, "So, what happened everyone ended up showing up to dinner last night?"

"Whenever I tell them I'm going to dinner with Alexz, at least one of them crashes our party. When Chad showed up and saw her boyfriend was there, he texted his brothers. Poor Alexz can't catch a break around us. However, her boyfriend was cool, and he expressed a desire to marry her. She's also pregnant with his baby. What gives Alexz pause is that he wants to accept a job in Atlanta. She ain't feeling the move."

"Oh wow! Congratulations! You're going to be a PaPa."

He chuckled as he opened his passenger door for me. "Thank you."

Once he closed the door, I put on my seat belt and waited for him to join me. I had a feeling why she didn't want to move, but I'd wait on him to tell me. Once he got inside and had cranked up, he said, "She doesn't want to leave me and her brothers, so I'm going to have to have a heart-to-heart with her. She mainly doesn't want to leave me. To prove to her that I will be fine, I would love for you and DJ to join us for Sunday dinner. Jamel, too, if he's going to be in town."

"Wow. Absolutely. Well... I say absolutely for me. I'll check with DJ, although I'm sure he will be there. I'm not sure if Jamel is going to make the drive down since he's still having some issues with his arm, but I'll mention it."

He backed out of his parking spot, and as he left the parking lot, "What Cha' Gonna Do for Me" came on the radio. I couldn't help but groove to it. I hadn't heard it in years. That was one of my favorite Chaka Khan songs. Sheldon glanced over at me as he drove, and a smirk formed on his lips. "I'm gon' do whatever you want me to do, beautiful," he said, answering the question Chaka Khan had posed in the song.

I bit my bottom lip as I stared at him. He was going to make me regret everything I'd told him about moving slowly. *Damn, Sheldon.* Him being so fine didn't help matters. His golden-brown skin with the light freckles on his cheeks and perfectly shaped lips made me want to do things to him that I hadn't done to anyone in years. I reached over and slid my hand over his gray beard and watched him bite his bottom lip as I had done.

"Sheldon, are you trying to seduce me?"

"Not at all, baby. That song is doing it for me."

He chuckled as I admired his high cheekbones. I smiled back and slowly shook my head. He was right though. I was posing the question. There was no way I would leave for New Orleans without him if he still wanted to come with me. Sheldon was so easy going and open—the total opposite of what he was when I first met him.

We continued to the restaurant, enjoying the music, and when he turned in the parking lot, he said, "I look forward to spending time with you. It's the highlight of my day."

"I look forward to it too. So why don't you come with me to New

Orleans? I would probably be on the phone with you most of the time I was away anyway." I looked away as he parked then turned back to him. "I know I said that we should move slow, but you're so magnetic. I don't know how I would resist wanting to be around you."

He grabbed my hand and kissed it, sending chills on an excursion throughout my body. "I would love to accompany you to New Orleans. I'm glad you're having a change of heart. Honestly, I feel like you're my woman already. I know you're religious, so I'ma quote the bible a bit for you. Doesn't it say to call those things that be not as though they were?"

I slowly nodded as I stared at him. He was so sexy, and, in this moment, he was even sexier. I knew where he was going with this, and although he was quoting scripture, I was so turned on by his words. He continued with what he was saying, although I already knew what he was about to say. "So if I'm gonna do that, that means I should start calling you mine... treating you like you're mine... and wait for the manifestation of that. Am I right, Anissa Berotte?"

My face had to have turned beet red, because it was hot as hell. Sheldon was claiming that I would be his wife. That was huge. He gently stroked my hand with his thumb then lifted it to my cheek and did the same. I leaned into his touch and said, "I suppose you're right. In that case... I can't wait to meet my bonus kids as their stepmom instead of just being DJ's mama."

He smiled big... the biggest I'd ever seen him smile. Instead of responding to me, he got out of the car and came around to my side to open my door. Once he'd helped me out, he pulled me to him, sensually staring into my eyes. I thought he was going to kiss me. His face was close to mine, but he was holding his position. "Let's go eat, wife."

I could have melted to the cement. Knowing that he saw a future with me was beyond exciting and new. It was refreshing to know that there were men left who weren't playing games... who knew what they wanted when they saw it... knew what they needed when they felt it and weren't afraid to manifest it. I lifted my hand to his cheek and gently stroked it as I stared back at the man that had to be sent to me straight from God himself.

He could no longer hold back. He lowered his face to mine and kissed my lips, allowing them to linger. My inner wild cat was dying to tear into him. After sliding his hand through my hair, he grabbed my hand and said, "You gon' make me lose the lil bit of restraint I have left."

I couldn't stop the smile that broke out on my face. After leaning into him for a second, I allowed him to lead me into the restaurant so we could enjoy our dinner.

12

Sheldon

As I finished cleaning up, the doorbell rang, then someone walked in. I knew it had to be one of my kids. It was Sunday, and we were having dinner here, as usual. However, Anissa, DJ, and Jamel would be joining us, so I wanted to make sure the house was spotless. Anissa had never been past the kitchen, and the past few days we'd spent together this week, we'd done so at her place. Surprisingly, we hadn't crossed into unchartered territory, although it had been extremely tempting to do so. I'd never met Jamel, but I was sure he would get along with Shyrón and Dylan since they were close in age.

As I made my way to the kitchen, I heard my baby girl talking quietly. I wasn't sure if she was on the phone or if she'd brought Knowledge along with her. When I entered and saw her on the phone, I was grateful she was alone. I needed to talk to her about dinner the other night. When she turned around and saw me, she ended her call. "Hey, Daddy."

"Hey, baby girl. How are you?" I asked then kissed her cheek and rested my hand on her stomach.

She chuckled then said, "I'm fine. What about you?"

"I'm okay. Actually, I'm glad you were first to get here, because I needed to talk to you."

"I already know what this is about. All of you seemed to enjoy Knowledge the other night. He's coming over. He had to stop by his office for some paperwork he forgot and go to the store."

"I think you should accept his proposal, baby."

Her eyes widened, and I could see them instantly get glossy. "Daddy—"

"No, listen. You have to live your life. I'm fine. I promise. Even if I weren't, I still have four knuckleheads here to keep me company. You don't have to worry about me. I can get a nonstop flight and be to you in two hours from Houston, so three hours tops if you include the drive to the airport. You are my baby girl, and while I'll miss you, you have to live your life."

She slid her hand down her face then huffed loudly. "Daddy, I still don't want to move. We've only been dating for a few months. What if I get out there, living with him, and hate it?"

"What if you love it? Life is about taking chances. How will you know if you don't go?"

"I just... I'm not sure if I want to trust him so much, so soon."

"You trusted him enough to have a baby by him."

"That was an accident. It shouldn't have happened. The condom was too damn small, but it was all we had at the moment. Stupid as hell," she said under her breath.

"That wasn't an accident. You're right. It was stupid as hell if you weren't sure about what you wanted. It seems that he's sure in what he wants though."

She looked away then sat at the table. I sat next to her, and she practically whispered, "What if I'm not a good mother? Or what if I die while in labor like my mother?"

"Baby, you can't let fear ruin your life or keep you from living it like I did. I'm finally able to move on. It hasn't been easy, not by a long shot, but I refuse to continue being miserable. Your mom is in heaven, and the years have flown by like its wings were on steroids. I've allowed fear and grief to practically consume me for almost twenty-five years. Don't be like me, sugar. I love you too much to allow something like that."

She fell into me and practically cried her eyes out... until the door opened and Shyrón walked in. She quickly lifted her head and wiped her face on my shirt. "Sorry, Daddy."

"It's okay. At least you don't have on makeup."

She looked over at me and smiled then spoke to Shy as she quickly stood and left the room. He made his way to me to shake my hand. "What's up? Everything okay?"

"Yeah. She just needed some reassuring about her relationship with Knowledge."

"Hmm. I don't know about that shit."

I frowned hard. Shyrón was the son I trusted the most to have an accurate scoop on somebody. Because he was a lawyer, he could investigate the shit out of anybody and anything. Knowledge seemed like a good guy on the surface, and Alexz was usually a pretty good judge of character. Maybe whatever Shyrón had to say was the reason she wasn't totally comfortable with moving. "What'chu talkin' 'bout, Shy?" I questioned.

He sat next to me where he could see whenever Alexz would reappear. "That nigga got another woman. She's in Atlanta, and she's pregnant too."

My eyebrows lifted in shock. "How do you know that?"

"I bugged that nigga's phone. When Chad texted me to say y'all were all at Saltgrass, I got to work. Plus... baby sis ain't no fool. She asked me to do a background check to make sure he wasn't in the system. I'm almost sure she wasn't banking on this shit though."

I nodded repeatedly. When his ass got here, it was gon' be some shit. "So what do you know about this other woman?"

He slid his hand down his mouth and slowly shook his head. "She's the same age as Alexz. She ain't got nothing really going for herself though... just depending on him to take care of her and their baby. This nigga wants them all to live together as a family but wasn't gon' spring that shit on Alexz until she was already in Atlanta. I ain't knocking nobody that's into that kind of shit, but you know as well as I do that Alexz ain't gon' be down with that."

"Hell naw. That nigga done lost his fucked-up mind if he think she gon' be cool with that shit. I hate she's pregnant for that muthafucka now. He should have been open and honest with her from jump."

"Yeah. That's the main reason he wants to accept the job in Atlanta. He can be close to his baby. She's having a boy and is due in July... less than two months from now. Alexz will bring the extra income to sustain them and get this... the nigga talking about finding another woman to bring into the picture as well. Alexz gon' flip."

"Shit. I'm on the verge of flipping. That nigga on his way. I know you can keep your cool, but don't tell Chad or Isaiah right now. Alexz needs to know first... but after dinner. We're gonna make it through this dinner since we will have guests, then we'll address it."

"I can keep my cool, but I'm gon' have to stay away from his ass. I won't be able to keep a straight face when I look at him," Shy said.

He stood from his seat and hugged Alexz. I'd never seen her enter the room. Standing from my seat, I went to the stove to check the smothered pork shoulder steak. Anger was flowing through me, and I just hoped I could contain myself when that nigga walked through the door. I didn't want Jamel to see this drama, because I wanted to get to know him first. However, DJ was familiar with how much we all protected Alexz, and I knew that Anissa would understand if anything popped off.

The others should be arriving soon, because I asked them to get here early so the meal would be complete before Anissa arrived.

Chad had done corn-on-the-cob and would pick up some Hawaiian rolls on his way. Isaiah would be bringing the green beans and red beans, and Dylan was bringing drinks. I didn't have Shyrón bring anything because I knew he'd had a long weekend preparing for a case. Alexz was supposed to be bringing desserts, but I didn't see the first cake or cookie come through the door when she arrived.

After making sure the meat wasn't sticking to the pot, I turned the fire off. The gravy was perfect, just in case someone wanted to skip the red beans and just eat rice and gravy. When I turned back to look at Shy and Alexz, I knew he was talking to her about his background check. He was speaking so quietly I'd never heard him. *Nigga couldn't hold water.* I knew I'd said to wait until after dinner to tell her.

Her face was red as hell, and she looked like she was about to blow a gasket. I walked over to them and sat in front of her. "After the dinner," I said then cut my eyes at Shyrón. "We will address that nigga after dinner."

"Why? If Anissa can't handle this shit, she won't be a good fit. We look out for each other, no matter what the situation, especially when it concerns Alexz."

I stood from my seat and looked at Shy in his eyes. "Let her get to know us first. That's why all of you are still single. Use some common sense. If she sees all of this before getting to know you, she will assume you are this way all the time. Once she knows who you are and what you stand for, *then* you can fuck somebody up in her presence. Now again, don't tell Chad and Isaiah."

I looked at my baby girl because she was quiet as hell. That wasn't like her. She normally was the loudest in the room when she was pissed. She wasn't pissed yet. She was hurt. Sitting next to her, I put my arm around her. After kissing her head, I said, "I'm sorry, baby."

"I need to have an abortion."

She said it so quietly. It killed my soul to hear her say that because I could hear the pain in her voice when she said it. "Alexz, you don't have to—"

"I cannot deal with his ass anymore after this. Having this baby would mean that he would be a part of my life whether I wanted him to be or not. He led me to believe that I was the love of his life... that I was his one and only. Fuck him!"

She grabbed her phone and made a phone call, but the person she called didn't answer. I supposed she was calling him. She threw her phone to the table and said, "How dare he think he would get away with some bullshit like this! You know I'm gon' fuck him up when he walks through that door, right?"

"No, you aren't. If I have to restrain you myself, you won't be in here trying to fight a man, especially not with five other men in this house."

Chad, Isaiah, and Dylan all walked in at the same time, carrying their contributions for today's dinner. Chad, the most intuitive, looked around the room and asked, "What the fuck happened?"

This wasn't going to be good. As I checked the time, I knew Anissa and her boys would be arriving any minute. They'd gone to church, and she usually got out about twelve thirty. It was twelve thirty now. I blew out an exasperated breath as Shy said, "That nigga a fraud ass muthafucka. That's what happened."

Dylan stopped putting drinks in the fridge, and Isaiah turned his attention to Shy as well. They all adorned frowns as I rolled my eyes. Alexz was pacing back and forth. "Yo! Alexz, what he talkin' 'bout?" Chad asked.

"I'm pregnant for a nigga that wants to have me living in some kinda fucking compound with sister wives and shit. Shy did a background check for me and found out the nigga has another woman in Atlanta that's pregnant too. He wants us all to live together, but he hasn't said a word to me about this shit. I'm too possessive for some shit like that. Fuck him."

Dylan's eyebrows lifted. "Damn. That sounds almost like my type of party, minus the pregnancies."

Everyone turned to him as he shrugged. However, his comment did just what it should have. Everyone's tension eased a bit as Chad looked at him and said, "Shiiid, not with a woman like Alexz. Imagine having to deal with her attitude times two."

"Naw, nigga, times three. He's looking for another woman to add to the stable," Shyrón clarified.

"That's some bullshit," Isaiah added. "So he never told you this shit? He was just gon' spring this shit on you if you moved?"

"Yeah. I'd been feeling uneasy about moving with him for so many reasons, but the biggest reason was that I didn't feel like I trusted him enough to leave everyone I knew and loved and totally commit to it being just me and him. Now I know why. It wasn't just me and him. Bitch-ass nigga."

I slowly shook my head as I stood to take plates from the cabinet. I could hear doors closing, so I knew Anissa had probably arrived. "Well, get ready to meet our new step-mama," Chad said. "She's here."

They chuckled a bit as Isaiah clapped my shoulder. "I'm happy for you, Dad. For real. It's about time."

I nodded. *It was time, and the right woman came along to show me that it was time. I had heaven here with me and didn't even know it.* Those were the words on my heart that I wanted to say, but my tongue froze, not wanting to express so much to my son.

Isaiah smiled and went to the cabinet to retrieve glasses as Chad opened the door for our guests. He and DJ barked loudly, and I rolled my eyes. Since they were both Q's, they did that shit every time they saw one another... at least in my presence. They probably did it because they knew it irritated me. Making my way to them, I saw the most beautiful woman enter the house. She wore a beautiful, knee-length wrap dress, showcasing her cleavage. Her hair was curly, and she'd worn her glasses. I loved her glasses. They were so sexy.

She smiled as soon as her eyes landed on mine. Thinking about the past few days with her had me feeling light and losing the heaviness from the conversation we were having before she arrived. Maybe everything would be cool. My sons seemed to have let it go for now. I knew once Knowledge arrived, that would be a different story. I leaned over and gave Anissa a soft peck on her lips. "Hey, baby."

"Hey," she responded as she began to redden. She turned to her son. "Jamel, this is my boyfriend, Sheldon. Sheldon, this is my youngest son, Jamel."

I shook his hand as he nodded. "Nice to meet you."

I nodded and said, "Same here. Come on in so I can introduce you to everyone."

He nodded as I glanced at the sling his left arm was in. I grabbed Anissa's hand and led them to the kitchen where everyone was. Chad and DJ were standing over the stove. "Get away from my pots, you buzzards!"

Everyone chuckled. DJ was like one of my sons. He was extremely comfortable at my house. "Everybody, this is Jamel, Anissa's son and DJ's younger brother. Jamel, the beautiful queen right there is my daughter, Alex with a Z. The wild and uncontained one at my stove is Chad, but I'm sure you already know him. This is Isaiah. He's the oldest and most reliable. That's Dylan over there. Most times, he's in his own world unless you pull him into yours, and lastly, this is Shyrón, the family attorney and gangsta."

Jamel chuckled at my introductions and the frowns on most of their faces. "What's up, everybody? Sounds like I'ma fit right in around here."

They all chuckled as they approached him to shake his hand and welcome him into the family it seemed. I slid my arm around Anissa then kissed her head. Once they were all done with their personal introductions, I got their attention again. "As you all know, this is Anissa. She's going to be around for a long time, so get used to it."

She blushed as Alexz smiled big and approached her with open arms. It was like all that bullshit hadn't happened earlier. She hugged her tightly and said, "Welcome to the family, Ms. Anissa. Finally! Now I have somebody I can go shopping with."

At that moment, I realized that my baby girl probably needed her just as much as I did. There were certain things she would probably feel more comfortable speaking to a woman about... things that only another woman would understand. I smiled as my crew welcomed her. Once they finished hugging her, I pulled her in my arms, as they all looked on, and kissed her lips. We stared into one another's eyes like we were the only ones in the room.

We spent the entire day together yesterday and the day before, shopping, talking, and cuddling. We watched movies, cooked, and I even helped her wash and detangle her hair. I knew that I could get so used to having her around me every day, all day. I wasn't one to play around with my emotions or anything that I wanted. She was who I wanted, and I knew that quickly. After one week, I knew I had everything with her. Counseling was going to be a breeze now, because I was so submerged in her I couldn't think about anyone else.

"Y'all can stare at each other all day, but we finna eat without y'all," Chad said loudly.

"Let them get full off love. I need food," DJ added.

Resting my forehead against Anissa's as she chuckled, I said, "Welcome home, baby."

13

Anissa

Sunday dinner was everything I knew it would be. Jamel had fit in perfectly like he'd known them all along. Although when we first walked in, I could feel the heaviness in the room, when Alexz's boyfriend walked in, it seemed to get even heavier. Everyone seemed to be ignoring him intentionally. They could be at ease around me. If I knew one thing, I knew that Sheldon was a good man and that he'd raised responsible and respectful adults. I understood their family dynamic because ours was similar. They looked out for each other.

When he walked in with ice cream and cake, Alexz had turned completely red. I wasn't sure what was going on, but whatever it was, I knew it would possibly come to a head before I left. The tension in the room was only getting thicker the longer he was here. Alexz had sat next to me, engaging in conversation for at least thirty minutes.

She was planning outings for us like I was the mother she'd always craved. She was definitely the daughter I'd always wanted. I was just grateful they'd all accepted me as the woman in Sheldon's life without any fuss.

Dylan and Jamel seemed to hit it off the most. He'd talked to him more than anyone else. I knew for sure they had a couple of things in common. They both loved women, and they both needed Jesus. As I sat next to Sheldon, soaking up his aura, my cell phone rang. The number was unknown. Normally, I didn't answer those, but since Sheldon had noticed it ringing, I answered it. I didn't want him to think I was hiding anything. "Hello?"

"Hey, Anissa. It's Yolanda. I've been trying to call you, but I assume you blocked me. I'm so sorry. I really want to talk to you. Can you meet me somewhere?"

I rolled my eyes as Sheldon clowned around with Chad and DJ, not noticing my annoyance with the call I was on. "Yolanda, what is there to talk about? You brought bullshit to my doorstep," I said as I stood from my seat.

That seemed to get quite a few people's attention. I pulled the phone from my ear and said to everyone, "I apologize for my language. I need to take this call outside."

Before I could walk away, Sheldon grabbed my hand. "You okay?"

"Yeah. It's Yolanda. This won't take long."

He nodded and released me from his grasp. Bringing the phone back to my ear, I said, "You have no right to call me. I blocked you for a reason. There is no excuse that you can come up with that will be good enough, Yolanda. One thing that has developed better than anything in my fifteen years of being single and dealing with foolery is my cut-off game, especially within the past couple of years."

"You're right. I have no logical excuse. I was being sneaky and underhanded, knowing I was fooling around with someone else's man and playing with fire. I'm sorry I involved you in my bullshit. I really am. I'm most sorry for losing a real friend. You've been there for me more than anyone else for the past year and a half, and I appreciate you so much for that. God, that was so stupid. I love you, Anissa."

She ended the call, and just hearing the desperation in her voice had softened me. It was foul for her to give out my address that way to benefit her scheming ass, but she got caught up. I knew what that was like. I was caught up with Sheldon, and I hadn't even experienced his loving yet. We all did stupid mess where a man was concerned. After taking a deep breath, I called her back. The phone rang a few times then went to voicemail. I unblocked her number and called that line, only to suffer the same fate.

I decided to send a text message to both numbers. *I love you too, Yolanda. I'm sorry for losing my cool. I was just so angry because my peace is everything to me. I got a taste of it a year and a half ago and I don't want to ever let go of it again. You threatened that. But I forgive you. Call me back and we can set up a time to meet and talk.*

Hopefully, she would call me back. Again, there was no excuse for what she did, but maybe she needed a listening ear. Thankfully, everything turned out okay for me when that woman showed up at my door. That was the only reason she was getting a chance to explain. I tried to be forgiving, but had I gotten hurt, God would have had to *really* work on me about her. I would have beat her ass.

༺༻

THE DAY WAS WINDING DOWN, AND I WAS READY TO GO HOME and relax. Alexz's boyfriend, whose name I learned was Knowledge, had spent a lot of time talking to Jamel. He didn't seem to notice that no one else was really talking to him. If he did notice, he didn't care. Just as I was about to tell Sheldon we were going to head out, Knowledge got everyone's attention. *Lawd have mercy.* I could feel that this wasn't going to be good.

He smiled like all was well and turned his attention to Alexz. The scowl she had on her face reminded me of Gabrielle Union's scowl in the movie *Deliver Us from Eva*. That alone should have made him rethink whatever it was he was about to say in front of everybody. Despite all the frowns and Alexz's facial expression, his clueless ass continued. "I just want to thank all of you for accepting me into the family, and thank you, baby, for introducing me to your people. I see where you get your strength from."

Shyrón turned his head, and since he had the lightest complexion of the brothers, his annoyance was more visible through his red face. DJ seemed to know something, too, because he looked just as angry as everyone else. Sheldon didn't have a frown, but he didn't look excited either.

"Alexzandria, you are everything I've been missing in my life, and now that you are having my baby, it solidifies our connection. I love you with everything in me."

When he went to his knee, my eyebrows rose. All four of her brothers and DJ stood from their seats, and Sheldon sat up, scooting to the edge of his seat. Alexz stood from her seat as Knowledge smiled at her. "Alexzandria Marie Berotte, will you be my wife?"

"Hell naw!" Shyrón yelled, catching him off guard.

He looked toward him with a frown on his face then gaged the entire room. When his eyes met Alexz's, she said, "Fuck yo' cheating, conniving ass! How the fuck you was gon' get me to Atlanta and then tell me about the other woman pregnant for you that you wanted me to live with like a fucking sister wife and shit? Get the fuck outta here with that shit!"

She slapped the ring from his hand as he stood, and he almost looked like he wanted to hit her. I was so damn nervous. While I knew that no one in this room would allow him to hurt anyone, I worried about what would happen when she would be alone... whether he would be stupid enough to try something with her then. "Alexz, I think it's a doable situation. You are still the only woman I love. I haven't slept with her since I met you, so I didn't cheat, baby."

"You may not have cheated sexually, but you definitely cheated in other ways. You're a deceitful, conniving ass nigga. I knew it was something about you that I felt like I couldn't trust. I'm glad I had my brother look into your ass. I'm not having this baby."

He took a step toward her, and even Jamel stood from his seat in a protective stance. I was the only one still seated as Sheldon approached him. "What's on your mind? We were trying to let you make it out of here, but you got a lil bit too much hostility in you when you look at my daughter. She didn't do a damn thing wrong. You did. If you don't get your fraud ass out of here, I'm gon' unleash these hounds on yo' ass. I'm the only reason why they haven't attacked you yet."

"You got sixty seconds to get the fuck out of here," Shyrón added as he placed a hand to Chad's chest to restrain him.

I swore I heard Chad growl like a damn dog. This was about to get ugly if he didn't get out of here. I stood and went over to Alexz to try to calm her down. She looked like she was about to jump over her dad to get to him. When I grabbed her hand, I could feel the tremble in it. "Come on, Alexz. He's not worth it, baby."

She looked over at me, and I could see the tears that were threatening to fall from her eyes. She sucked her emotions up and looked back at Knowledge. There was so much hostility in her. She slid her hand from mine, and she moved so fast, I barely saw her. She knocked the piss out of him. Her brothers immediately collapsed on him, making sure he didn't even try to retaliate as Sheldon snatched her up and walked toward the back.

She was kicking and screaming, clearly wanting to cause even more damage. When they stood Knowledge to his feet, he had blood coming from his mouth. The frown on his face was deep as hell, but he kept his cool. He knew better. They'd kill him in here. He spit something in his hand, and I realized that she'd knocked his tooth out. *Shit!* He turned to walk out before anyone could further mess him up. Alexz grew up with boys and was raised by a man, so I wasn't in the least bit surprised that she could do that sort of damage.

As he left, Chad, DJ, and Shyrón followed him out. "This shit is fucked up. That nigga had to have known that something was up.

With as much as we talked to him the other night at dinner, then to get here and nobody was saying anything, he had to be slow," Dylan said.

"Jamel distracted him," Isaiah added. "Had he not had anyone to talk to, he would have realized it."

"You think? I mean... damn. I know he saw all the mean mugs on our faces when he stood up there trying to propose. Hell, he had to have seen Alexz's face. She was looking like she wanted to stab that nigga."

I stood from my seat to go check on Sheldon and Alexz, but before I got to them, I heard a scuffle outside. I quickly ran to the door to see that Shyrón had him jacked up against the car. DJ seemed to be trying to talk him out of doing something he might regret while Chad was doing the opposite. When Shy let him go, he got in his car and left. They all quickly made their way inside. "Is everything okay?" I asked.

"He talking about taking my sister to court to keep her from having an abortion. That nigga don't want none of this," Shy said as he knocked some papers off the countertop.

I was quickly learning that the one who was the most educated had the worst temper. He was the most hood out of all of them, and I wondered if he'd gotten that from Sheldon or their mother. My instincts told me it was Sheldon though. He wasn't around his mother long enough to pick up on any of her ways. Sheldon had said that Shyrón was only four years old when she died. *Maybe that indeed was enough time to pick up on personality traits.*

Going to him, I sat beside him at the bar. He looked up at me, and the hardened expression on his face softened some. "I'm sorry you had to witness this, Ms. Anissa. I just love my family. If anyone wants to push my buttons, all they have to do is mess with one of them. Otherwise, I'm a pretty laid back guy."

"It's okay. I totally understand. People can be so selfish and self-absorbed. It's sickening that he would try to deceive her that way."

He grabbed my hand and squeezed it slightly then made his

way to the room where Dylan, Jamel, and Isaiah were seated. Chad and DJ were still outside talking. As I stood from my seat to put food in the fridge that we'd put in containers earlier while cleaning the kitchen, Sheldon appeared behind me. He slid his arms around my waist and said in my ear, "I'm sorry. We did our best to hold in all this turmoil today. We'd done well until that raggedy ass proposal."

I closed the refrigerator and turned to him, bringing my hands to his cheeks. "It's okay. I don't know how y'all were able to restrain yourselves, knowing what he was trying to do to Alexz."

"I told them that we couldn't show out in front of our guests."

He chuckled after saying it as I twisted my lips to the side. "I had a whole crackhead for an ex-husband. I have seen a little bit of everything. Thankfully, he's clean now, but the turmoil I went through with him almost broke me. I would not have judged y'all based on how you responded to what Knowledge was trying to do."

Chad and DJ walked inside, and they both gave us a head nod and went to the room with everyone else. Turning my attention back to Sheldon, I asked, "How's Alexz?"

"Mike Tyson is in there with everyone else, with ice on her hand."

I chuckled as he pulled me close. "I know we're supposed to be leaving for New Orleans tomorrow, but I may need to stay behind."

My heart sank a bit, but I understood his concern for his daughter. I slid my hands up his chest as I stared at it and said, "I understand."

He grabbed my hand and kissed it then led me to the room with everyone. As I was about to sit, he pulled me close to him. "So tomorrow, Anissa and I were set to go to New Orleans. Actually, it was her trip, and I was just crashing it. Considering today's events, I think I'm going to stay home and make sure everything is straight."

Oh, that was smart. I saw exactly what he was doing. He knew they would literally force him to go. While I knew he wanted to be here for his daughter, I also knew that he didn't want to miss our trip.

Just as I knew they would, they all started speaking at once, telling him to go.

"Daddy, I still have to work tomorrow. Despite the shit I put my hand through, I will be there bright and early. If it's still swollen, I'll get it looked at."

"You knocked that nigga tooth out. You might have broken your shit. We ought to get it checked out now. You can come to work with me tomorrow if necessary. The kids will be excited to meet my lil sister," Dylan said.

"You know you'd be able to come with me. I have court tomorrow, but you could sit in."

Alexz fake yawned as Shyrón talked, causing everyone to laugh. Once they stopped laughing, Sheldon asked, "Are you sure? You know you my baby."

"Daddy, seeing you this happy with a woman is what all of us have always wanted. To know that you've found that brings me joy. Honestly, I think I needed some estrogen around here as much as you did. Go to New Orleans and enjoy yourself. Shyrón and I have to prepare for my defense anyway... just in case that fool tries to get at me for assault."

Sheldon slowly shook his head then pulled me to the couch. When I leaned into him, he nuzzled his nose to my ear and said, "It's me and you for three days. I can't wait."

I lifted my head to stare into his eyes. "I can't wait either."

14

Sheldon

When we arrived at the Intercontinental Hotel in the French quarter, I got out of the car and stretched. The four-hour drive wasn't bad with Anissa by my side. We didn't stop once. We'd gotten breakfast from Whataburger before we left, and that had held us over. I was starving now though. Going around to her side of the car, I opened the door for her and assisted her from her seat. Watching her in the flowy, sheer top and tight capri pants she wore was a sight to behold. She had her long hair in a ponytail today and had worn her shades. She looked to be glowing, and I hoped as long as she was with me, she would stay that way.

After getting our luggage and going inside to get checked in, I planned to take her for lunch at Beaucoup Eats. Afterward, we'd just walk the streets to see what we could get into later. I felt alive again, and for that, I owed her the world. After yesterday, I could use a getaway. It took a lot of restraint not to kick that nigga in his mouth while he was on his knee proposing to my daughter. It had taken a lot of restraint for everyone.

However, Alexz's restraint crumbled, and she almost caused everyone else's to crumble as well. I was worried about her though. The hurt I saw in her eyes had my heart heavy. Although she wasn't crying, I knew she would cry as soon as she was alone. When I took her to her old bedroom, she lay in the bed and just stared at the ceiling. Her breathing was heavy, and I knew she needed peace. I scheduled her a massage for later today and kissed her cheek, assuring her that we would all be there for her.

Heartbreak was never a good feeling, and with as hard as she pretended to be, I knew this was eating her alive. All my children had pieces of me in them, but one of the pieces she had was suppressing her feelings. I'd done it for years. I refused to do that any longer, and I needed her to see that it wasn't healthy for her or the baby she was carrying. I didn't know whether she would actually go through with having an abortion or not. Whatever she chose to do, I would be there for her.

After getting to our room, we both fell onto the bed at the same time. I smiled at Anissa as she giggled. It was going to be amazing being with her... and for three days. If I didn't have to make it back to my counseling session on Thursday, we would probably stay longer. She rolled over on her side and stared at me for a moment. As she propped her head on her hand, she said, "I tried so hard to resist you, but God, you're so... gorgeous. Your spirit has swallowed me whole, Sheldon. I don't know how you did that and within a week, but I'm happy to be here with you."

I turned my body to her and gently caressed her cheek with my thumb. "I don't know how you did it either. I can't seem to function now without you. Those three days were hell on me. Although I was the one that stopped talking, you were all I thought about... you and Marie. I had to come to grips with the fact that I fulfilled my vows to her. I was an amazing husband. I wasn't perfect, but I loved her perfectly. I want to love you perfectly too. I haven't known you long, and I know I still have so much to learn about you, but I feel as if you deserve everything I have to offer plus some."

She blushed as I stared at her. "This is unreal," she practically whispered.

"Tell me about it."

I rolled back to my back, and she scooted closer to me and rested her head on my shoulder. It was like now that we had the time to do whatever we wanted to do, we were content just being in one another's presence without interruptions. Neither of us were close to our extended families, and I thought that was weird for both of us. She was an only child but had a host of cousins. I had a brother, but we rarely talked. So for us to find one another had to be destined by God.

My stomach growled loudly, and I couldn't help but chuckle. She did, too, then sat up. "I suppose we should get something to eat before your stomach gets really angry."

"Yeah. I'm taking you to Beaucoup Eats. They have a variety of food, so I'm sure you will find something appealing to your appetite."

I sat up from the bed and helped her to her feet as well, and our bodies ended up pressed together. My breathing became a little heavier as my dick started to rise. Feeling her body against mine always did that to me. She licked her lips and slid her arms around my waist. I closed my eyes for a moment as I slid my hands down her back. *Damn this was hard.* I didn't want to pressure her into sex, but if we kept having moments like this, I would have to take initiative and see where we ended up.

Something told me that she would be down for whatever I wanted to do. She slowly pulled away from me, and we silently left the room to head to lunch at Beaucoup.

After feeling like we'd walked nearly all of Canal and Bourbon Streets, we made our way back to our hotel to shower and relax until dinner time. Shit, after all the walking, I'd definitely worked up my appetite all over again. Before long, Anissa would be hearing my stomach growl. I'd held her hand and constantly showered her with affection all day, and I couldn't wait to hold her in my arms.

I rummaged through my luggage to get a t-shirt and some shorts out. Anissa had unpacked and used the drawers, but I was the type to live out of my suitcase. She'd tried to convince me to unpack as well, but I just couldn't fathom putting my clothes in dresser drawers for only a couple of days. A couple of weeks? Possibly.

Once I got what I needed, I started the shower in the bathroom. When I came back to the room, I found Anissa doing the same. "You wanna shower first, baby?"

She glanced up at me, and a chill slithered down my spine. She didn't answer me, so I walked closer to her as she stared at me. I refused to assume what I felt I knew was happening. I needed her to verbalize her wants and desires. When I got to her, I said, "Or we can shower together, if that's something you want to experience."

I allowed my gaze to slide up and down her body, then I pulled her close and leaned over to kiss her neck. When I felt her shiver, I pulled away some. Anissa stared at me for a little longer, then she slowly lifted her shirt and pulled it off. When she threw it to the countertop and turned back to me, she took off her bra. *Damn.* I wanted to pull her nipples into my mouth immediately, but I felt like I needed to be more patient with this process.

Doing as she had done, I slowly pulled my shirt and undershirt over my head as well. Her shallow breathing pulled me toward her along with seeing the hardness of her nipples. I grabbed her by the back of her neck and slowly pulled her to me. I wanted to be gentle, but everything in me wanted to ravage her body like a starved lion.

I'd gone without sex for so damn long, just the anticipation of it had me about to nut. I didn't know how I managed to go without it for all these years, but I could only hope that it was still in tip top shape.

At fifty-five years old, I knew that some things had most likely changed, but I hoped that wasn't one of them.

I inhaled the scent of her hair then lowered to her ear. "Damn, Anissa. You so damn beautiful."

I grabbed her earlobe with my teeth and watched the goosebumps appear on her shoulder. She slid her hands up my arms then around my neck as I circled an arm around her waist. "I've been wanting this since the first time I saw you, Sheldon. Everything about you rocked me from the very beginning. Be gentle with me at first. Once I get acclimated, please take me however you want me."

My dick was hard as a rock, so I was glad that she would be okay with me eventually getting forceful, because I was going to need all that action. The things I'd seen in pornos had me wishing I had someone to try them on. Marie and I didn't deviate much from the normal. She wasn't as risky with certain things, but what we had was pure, and neither of us felt like we were missing out on anything.

Pulling away from Anissa, I stared into her eyes as I unbuttoned her jean capri pants. When I felt her tremble, I quickly laid my lips on hers, doing my best to relax her body to receive me. I didn't even know if we would make it to the shower before I had my first taste of her. Sliding my hands in her waistband and around to her ass, I gripped it while letting out a slight moan. God, it had been so long. The only thing that was keeping me sane was knowing that it had been a long time for her too.

Backing up slightly, I pulled her pants off, and she stepped out of her sandals as well. I grabbed her hand as I stood back up and slowly spun her around, getting a glimpse of her in all her glory. Her ass had swallowed the thong she wore, and I could imagine how soaked the crotch of them were.

When she was facing me again, I went to my knees and kissed her stomach. Her light complexioned skin had a red hue, and I knew it was because of what I was doing to her. I wanted her to experience a high like no other, so whatever I had to do to assure that, I would do. After placing kisses in various places, I pulled her thong from her hips down her legs. I kissed her mound, but that was only teasing myself. I wanted the whole damn pie. Just the thought of having her cream on my lips and tongue had my mouth watering.

While I was on my knees, I pulled my shorts and drawers off, stretching them over my dick. My shit was becoming painful, and I knew I would have to put him out of his misery soon. Once I stood back up, my shorts and drawers dropped to my feet, and Anissa immediately grabbed my dick. I almost nutted just from her touch. I had to close my eyes and bite my bottom lip as I regained control.

She began stroking him, and I almost couldn't take the shit. I grabbed her by her neck, watching her head drop back. Her moans were only fueling my fire. I stooped slightly and picked her up. "Wrap your legs around me, Nissa."

I descended upon her nipple and gently grazed it with my teeth as I sucked it into my mouth. She held on to me tightly as I walked to the bed, ready to slide into her paradise. The heat coming from her was doing nothing to stifle my desire. My dick was leaking and throbbing with anticipation... drooling at the fact that her pussy was so close, and he still wasn't inside of her.

When I got to the bed, I laid her on it then slid on top of her. I continued my assault on her nipples as she held my head in her hands, being sure to give them an equal amount of attention. "Sheldon, please. Oooh. I need you now."

"Can I enter you raw?" I asked, hoping she said yes.

I hadn't worn a condom in so damn long that shit would probably make me go soft. "Mm hmm. Just give it to me."

She didn't have to beg me. Without even looking down, my dick knew exactly where that heat was coming from. Slowly, I breached her opening, and her nails dug into my flesh. She was like a virgin all over again. I just knew she'd had a dildo or something that she played with, but with as tight as she was, I knew that I'd been the only thing to enter her sanctuary in a long time. I pulled out of her only to reenter her again.

I pushed in a little further as I watched her wince, but I held my position as my dick twitched inside of her. He had to be making himself comfortable in there, because I wouldn't be able to do without her after this. As the look of pain eased from her face, I gave her more and began stroking her. I wasn't going to last long. There was no way. I could feel my nut rising already. "Ohhh, Sheldon, this feels so damn good."

"Mmm. Yes, it does, but I'm not going to last this round, baby."

"Just give me the best you have for the time we have left. We have all day."

When I thrusted inside of her, giving her all of me, it seemed she stopped breathing for a moment. I hadn't given her all of me before now, because I wasn't sure if she could handle it. However, with as good as she felt, I needed to know if I could be completely free to fuck her world up. As I held my position, I kissed her neck. After she wrapped her legs around me, I knew she was ready for me to keep going. I stroked her slowly, doing my best to hold off my nut, but it was getting harder with every second. "Sheldon... yeeeessss, baby."

That was all she had to say to have me increasing my pace a bit. However, when her walls put that death grip on me, that was it. "Shit! I'm cumming, baby!" she screamed as she practically convulsed beneath me.

I fired off inside of her, silently praying that my dick didn't fail me after this. She wrapped her arms around my neck and held me close to her. Her body was still jerking somewhat, and that let me know that I'd aced the assignment. It was both of our first experience in years, and it was amazing. "Damn, Anissa. Shit."

I couldn't even form an intelligible thought, let alone a sentence. My nerves were all exposed, and my body was tingling. When I slid out of her, it produced a shiver throughout my entire being. Standing from the bed, I helped her up and led her to the shower before the water got cold. We were both silent, I suppose thinking about the territory we'd just crossed into. That moment had heightened my feelings for her. Our connection was intense before sex, but now I knew that we were compatible in every way.

As we got in and stood under the spray, I wrapped my arms around her waist and kissed her neck. She turned to me and said, "Sheldon, that was even more than what I expected. Damn."

As she voiced her satisfaction, my dick began rising to the occasion again, and I thanked God for his grace and mercy. I grabbed her towel and began washing her from head to toe. I wanted to taste every inch of her when we got out of here. She kept her eyes on me as I washed her, and that shit kept my erection strong as hell. She was so damn sexy without even trying to be. I believed that was what turned me on about her the most.

After I'd slid the towel on almost every part of her, I rinsed it out to be sure I didn't put an abundance of soap in my new playpen. That shit had quickly become my happy place. Before cleaning between her legs, I stared at her to see she was staring at my dick. "You like what you see, baby?"

"Mm hmm," she said softly as I dipped to clean her sweet spot.

The moan that left her made my dick jump. "Nissa, you keep making sexy ass sounds like that, we gon' end up ordering in."

She reached out and grabbed my dick as she said, "And you'll hear no objections from me."

I had to hurry up and clean myself so I could indulge in her. After I finished washing her and began cleaning myself, she moved behind me, putting her arms around me and sliding her nails down my chest and abs. She was gonna have me painting the walls of this shower instead of the walls of her pussy.

"Hand me the towel, and I'll wash your back."

I turned and gave it to her. The desire present in her eyes made me wanna take her right here in this shower. I was so damned pressed, I started stroking my dick. I needed to feel her insides immediately. I was already a fiend of her gushy shit, and I wasn't ashamed of it either. When she finished washing my back and had given me the towel back, I washed my dick. After rinsing it off, I turned my back to the spray to rinse it off. Anissa stared at me for a moment as I admired her body.

Just as I was about to pull her body to mine, she went to her knees and pulled my dick into her mouth. I wasn't expecting that type of action, but I was happy as hell to be getting it. She wasn't in the least bit shy about what she wanted, and I loved that. While I knew she could be reserved at times, that reservation didn't accompany her to New Orleans.

She pulled it from her mouth and lifted it to suck my balls. There was no way I'd be able to remain standing in this shower if I busted a nut down her throat. But shit... I didn't want to stop her either. She was about to get the savage side of me, though, if she kept handling me this way. She covered my dick with her mouth again as she stared up at me. Those dreamy eyes were taking me far away from here, and if she kept sucking me the way she was, she would get the excitement from my travels.

"Anissa, fuck!" I verbalized as I put my hands to her cheeks.

Slowly sliding my dick in and out of her mouth, I watched her close her eyes and moan while she took at least half my dick in her mouth. She brought her hand to the base of it and began stroking the parts she couldn't reach. I swore I'd levitated. When she gagged on my dick, practically coughing on it, I almost let go. Snatching her up from the floor, I picked her up and left the shower.

Going straight to the vanity, I sat her on it and went to my knees, giving her pussy my tongue. I licked it from her asshole to her clit then took it into my mouth as I savored her flavor. I sucked her like my life depended on it. I needed to be back inside of her as quickly as possible. I felt like I wouldn't be able to breath until my dick slid between her walls again. I inserted two of my fingers while she squirmed and moaned.

She pushed my face deeper into her as I stroked her g-spot and ate her shit like it would be my last meal. When her back arched, I knew that she was about to baptize me, and I was ready to feel the anointing all over my tongue and face. When she detonated, she released my head and grabbed her nipples. As I glanced up at her sex faces, I couldn't help but be in awe of her beauty.

As her tremors died down, I lifted my face from the best conditioner my beard had ever had and ran my hands down it. I watched her pant for a moment and play with her nipples, taking mental snapshots to remember her body as it was. I was about to ravage the fuck out of it.

15

Anissa

"Sheldon! Oh shit!"

The way he was stroking me had me trying to get away from him. I had never known such pleasure. It felt like I was having constant orgasms, and I didn't know how much longer I could handle it. He'd eaten me out expertly, and now he had me in the doggystyle position, pounding into me like heaven was attached to my cervix. The tender version I had of him earlier was nowhere to be found, but I was happy that he enjoyed me so much that I brought the beast out of him.

He leaned over and bit my shoulder then pulled my hair loose, making me feel sexier with every blow he delivered. Being with him in this way was something I had been imagining, but I would have never thought it would happen this soon. His words had penetrated my soul, and his presence rocked my entire existence. This man was the real deal, and his actions from the past few days were proving just that.

I never believed in love at first sight, but Sheldon had made a believer out of me. The care he showed me said that he loved me, and he'd have to do more than ghost me to prove otherwise. This was freedom and trust. When he told me he hadn't had sex since before his wife died, I believed him. He had no reason to lie to me. I hadn't been celibate for fifteen years, because I'd allowed Dexter to come back a couple of times, but he was still the only man I'd been with until now. The last time with him had been a few years ago.

Since I had already gone through menopause, and I trusted Sheldon, there was no need in prolonging what we both wanted because neither of us had a condom. I was happy that I didn't miss this opportunity of getting my back blown out for something we didn't necessarily need. What I did need and would need was to feel his dick inside of me on the regular. Just the power of it had my mouth dirtier than ever and saying words I hadn't said in a long time.

He slid his hand to my neck and the other to my breast as he rested his weight on top of me. Slowing his assault, he stroked me passionately as he moaned in my ear. His moans were so damn sexy. It was hard to believe he'd been able to keep all this passion to himself for nearly twenty-five years. I supposed his heart knew what and who he wanted. It felt good as hell to know that after all that time, I was the woman he found worthy of sharing a love he'd reserved for his deceased wife.

I turned my head to look into his eyes, and he immediately kissed my lips. Feeling his body glide up and down on top of mine was so sensual, and my orgasm was about to come down once again, although my body hadn't fully lost the effects of the last one. "Sheldon... I'm about to cum again, baby. Ahhh..."

"Mmm... give it to me, Anissa. Give me all of it."

I didn't have to give him a thing. He was taking just what he wanted, and I wasn't angry about it. My body was actually overwhelmed by it all. I hadn't even used a dildo in the past few years, so his dick nearly tore me apart at first entry. But now... Jesus... now, he could fuck it all up. It felt like he was made for me, and I couldn't get enough of him.

My orgasm ripped through me, and I nearly blacked out. I was dizzy as hell like I was high. I supposed I *was* high... high off everything he'd done to me thus far. He lifted his body and rolled his hips harder. I knew he was about to reach his climax as well. "Fuck! I love this pussy, woman. Shit!"

When he gripped my hips tightly, I knew his moment of reckoning had come. There was no way I could ever let go of this. Sheldon was the man I was supposed to do the rest of my life with. Although my marriage to Dexter didn't work out, I believed that he was meant for me for a season. When circumstances caused him to lose sight of what was important, our season had indeed passed.

Sheldon rolled off me to the bed as he softly panted. After a few moments, he turned to his side and stroked my cheek. He licked his lips and said, "You are amazing. My heart was filled with anger and sadness, but you made my love come down, and now that shit on replay. I couldn't be more grateful to be able to live again. I see us being together for the long haul, so I can only hope you have the same vision. I'm not going anywhere, Anissa."

"Neither am I, Sheldon. Get used to me being all in your space."

"Like I said yesterday, welcome home, baby."

"Thank you for meeting me."

I nodded. Sitting next to Yolanda on this park bench had my skin crawling, but I knew I needed to hear her out. She'd called me while Sheldon and I were still in New Orleans, asking for a meet up, and I agreed. I crossed my arms over my chest as I waited for her to explain what could have possibly been on her mind for her to give out my address for her foolishness.

"I met Kline two years ago. We both agreed that it would only be a sexual thing between us. My baby had just graduated from high school, and I was ready to let my hair down. So that was what it has been. Like most women in these types of situations, I got caught up. The dick was so damn good. He had a girlfriend when we met, but I didn't find out until a few months later when I saw him in the grocery store with her and their child."

His girlfriend was wrong in her timing when she said they'd just met. This had been going on for a while. "Yolanda, but why give him my address?"

"It had been two months since I'd seen him. I was desperate. I'd never allowed him to come to my house because of this very thing. We usually met at a hotel. I was thinking that if he got caught, she wouldn't find me, and it would all be a misunderstanding. I'd sent him pictures... nudes and other nasty shit where she could see my face. I'd been begging for some of his time, and when he told me he would meet me later that night, I jumped on it. She just happened to see it before he did. It was selfish as hell, Anissa. I'm so sorry. I know of your situation with your ex and how you don't like people at your place. I wasn't even thinking about that. I never thought she would actually pop up at your place though."

I slowly shook my head as I watched the tears stream down her cheeks. With as long as it had taken her to respond to my text message, I was worried about her. I was her only friend, and while she messed up, I was okay. I felt like she was sincere in her apology and just wasn't thinking. "How old is he?"

"Twenty-seven."

"Come here, you damn cougar," I said and stretched out my arms.

She chuckled as she fell into me. I embraced her as I blew out a breath. She was like the little sister I never had. Little sisters were allowed to do stupid shit at times. "Thank you, Anissa. I promise not to do no stupid shit like that again. I've been so depressed about losing your friendship and hurting you. I would never intentionally hurt you. I wasn't thinking... well, I was thinking, but not about you. All I could see was his dick and how he would twist my insides out."

I rolled my eyes, but my mind went to Sheldon and how he'd done just that the entire time we were in New Orleans. The first night, we'd barely made it to dinner. The minute we got back to our room, we were stripping each other's clothes off. The next day, we stayed in our room recuperating and cuddling but hit the town that night. I got so drunk I barely remembered getting back to the hotel. However, I definitely remembered all the places he took my body when we got back.

When Yolanda sat up, she said, "I'm so happy to have you back in my life. This past week has been rough, and I've been miserable. Chandler has been trying to figure out what was up with me too. He's even threatened to come home to see about me."

"Well, tell him you're okay, and I got'chu."

I was ready to get back to Sheldon, so I stood, pulling her up with me. We walked hand in hand to our cars, enjoying the breeze. Sheldon had gone to counseling yesterday and had kind of kept to himself a bit. We talked by phone, but we didn't see one another. He messaged me first thing this morning, though, saying that he needed me at his house ASAP. I'd chuckled at his message and promised him I would be there after I talked to Yolanda on her lunch break.

He'd sent back sad faces and told me to prepare to stay and be catered to all night. He didn't have to worry about that. I would always keep an overnight bag with me, until our relationship progressed to a more serious level, and we moved in together. Yolanda broke our silence by asking, "How are things with you and Sheldon?"

"They're great. We're a couple. When you called, we were in New Orleans."

"Oh wow! Congratulations! Y'all moved faster than I would have assumed you would have."

"Yeah. Faster than I ever thought we would too. I already know that he's the one I'm going to be with for the rest of my life."

"I'm so happy for you. Although you said you were content with being alone, I knew you craved love. Maybe I should be content with me too, huh?"

"Absolutely. How can you be happy with someone else unless you're happy with you? That would make you dependent on them for your happiness. The right person should add to it, but they shouldn't be the total source of it."

"You're right. I need to work on that. There is no way I can go as long as you did without sex though. I love it too much. However, my toys are going to get a workout for a little while."

I chuckled as I slowly shook my head. "I'll get with you tomorrow. Maybe you can come to Sunday dinner."

"I would like that. Thanks."

We hugged again, and I got in my car to head to Sheldon. I texted him to say I was on my way and asked if he needed me to get anything, but he didn't respond. Checking the time to see it was almost two o'clock, I shrugged and just headed his way. Jamming to my old school playlist, when "Love Come Down" came on, I thought about what Sheldon had said. He used those exact words our first night in New Orleans. *You made my love come down.*

My body heated up as I heard his voice in my head... his raspy, baritone voice. It wasn't terribly deep, but it was so sexy. *Was he saying he loved me already?* Maybe he was falling. I was sure he would be very clear whenever he told me he loved me. I wouldn't have to question anything. I was falling for him, that was for sure. He made it easy. How could I not fall?

When I pulled up to his house, my eyes widened. There were a couple of police cars, and I saw Sheldon in cuffs. My heart fell to my feet as I hurriedly got out of the car, running full speed in his direction. A police officer blocked me from getting to him. "That's my boyfriend! What happened? Sheldon!"

"Ma'am, can you please hold on for a moment. We're trying to figure out everything as well."

I stopped fighting him and took in my surroundings. Alexz was talking to an officer, and Shyrón was also cuffed. When the ambulance pulled up behind me, I knew this wasn't good. Dylan pulled in right behind them. Isaiah and Chad were probably still stuck at work. Chad would have a harder time leaving work since he was at the federal prison. They weren't even supposed to have their phones on them. I was dying to know what was going on. The paramedics raced by me and went to the back of the house.

"What's up, Ms. Anissa? What's going on?"

"I just got here, too, so I don't know yet."

He continued standing next to me, scoping out the scene. "It has to involve Knowledge. He's the only one that I can think of that would be here to get this reaction out of my dad and Shy."

He'd made a good point. After looking at Alexz again, I noticed she had a little blood on her arm, and she was holding it completely still. *Shit!* Apparently, Dylan noticed too, because he said, "Oh fuck no!" and tried to get closer, only for them to send him back toward me.

I brought my eyes back to Sheldon. Nothing about his facial expression said defeat. It was like he knew he would be let go. His frown was deep, and he looked satisfied with whatever had happened. When the paramedics came from the back, they had Knowledge on a gurney. He was bloody, but he was still alive. Both Shy and Sheldon must have been responsible for his current state if both of them were handcuffed.

I didn't see anything wrong with Sheldon, but I couldn't see his hands. Shy had a red spot in his face. This wasn't good. After loading Knowledge in the ambulance, the cops helped Sheldon and Shyrón to their feet and took them to two different cop cars.

Alexz finally made her way to me and Dylan. She needed to be going to the hospital as well though. "Alexz, what happened?" Dylan asked before she could quite reach us.

"Knowledge showed up here talking about getting a junction to keep me from having an abortion again. I don't know why he had to come here with that shit. He'd already said that Sunday when he left. When I lunged at him, he grabbed me by the arm and threw me to the ground. That was when Shy jumped him. Daddy was trying to see about me. When he punched Shy, Daddy got involved. This is so fucked up. I think my arm is broken."

"You need to get to the hospital, baby," I said as I watched the cop cars leave with Sheldon and Shy. "What did they say about your dad and brother?"

"They are taking them in, but most likely, they will be released. It's private property, and Knowledge was trespassing. Not to mention, they were defending me. You best believe I'm getting that abortion now. There's no way I can deal with him for years to come."

Another ambulance arrived, and a police officer as well as the paramedic approached. Dylan wrapped his arm around her shoulder as they escorted her to the ambulance. "Ms. Anissa, can you go to the police station? I got Alexz."

"Yes. I'll see y'all once I get your dad. Which hospital are y'all going to?"

"Baptist," Alexz said when Dylan had turned to her.

"Okay."

This shit was horrible. There was no way in hell Sheldon was going to allow Knowledge to come in here and hurt his daughter without consequence. That boy had to be a damn fool to think otherwise. Maybe he was hoping that Sheldon would have been the only one here with her. Even still, Sheldon worked out a lot. He wouldn't be an easy target.

As I drove to the station, I said a prayer that everything would work out. I couldn't have my man in jail over this foolery. Alexz was a beautiful woman, and I could see how that would make Knowledge crazy, but the boy had to have some crazy in him before he even met her for him to take things this far. All of this could have been prevented had he just been honest with her from the beginning.

They probably wouldn't have been together, but at least all of this wouldn't have occurred.

Once I got to the station, I let the cop up front know who I was here for then had a seat. I didn't know what would happen once they released Sheldon and Shy. We would obviously go check on Alexz, but I knew there would be more fallout about Knowledge before this was all said and done.

16

Sheldon

When I walked out of that police station, checking on Alexz was the first thing on my agenda. However, when I saw Anissa sitting there, waiting for me and Shyrón, all the aggression and hostility I felt was long gone. She ran to me and hugged me tightly. After she released me, she even hugged Shy. Once we left the confines of the police station and were outside, Shy said, "I'm so pissed, if I could get to him now, I would probably kill him."

"Well, calm down, son. You don't need to destroy your career over a nigga like that. Had he died, you would have really had to put those degrees to use to get us off. Thank you, Anissa, for being here for us, baby."

"Of course. Where else would I be?"

I kissed her head as we approached her car then opened the driver door for her to get in. I'd never been arrested before, but I would do life for my daughter. When that fool got beside himself and started hollering at my baby, Shy and I were quickly making our way outside. However, before we could get to them, she lunged at that nigga and landed a few punches, one of them right in his eye. Alexz and Shy had the worst tempers of my kids. It didn't take much to set her off, and I attributed that to the fact that she grew up with four boys. She had to be able to hold her own.

When he threw her off him, Shy attacked his ass immediately, and I went straight to Alexz to make sure she was okay. She'd landed hard, and her arm was positioned awkwardly. When I saw the tears on her face, I made sure she wasn't dying, then I joined Shy in beating the fuck out of him. He'd gotten one good lick off on Shy, but once I joined, he didn't have a chance. One of my neighbors had to have called the police when they heard the yelling, because I sure as hell didn't call them.

My baby never even screamed for us to stop, so that was why I knew the police were called before that. We weren't doing any talking, just delivering blows to his body wherever they landed. Had the police not shown up, he would have died in my backyard, because neither of us were letting up until they arrived. After joining Anissa and Shy in the car, she grabbed my hand, and I jerked it back. My shit was swollen and throbbing.

Her eyes widened as she looked down at them. "You need ice."

"I need to get to my daughter. I'll get ice later."

I would take all her tender loving care as soon as I knew that my baby was going to be okay. Her arm had to be broken. It didn't look good. I knew we should have gone outside with them, but we were trying to give them their privacy and not interfere in their personal affairs. I didn't know what he was thinking by slinging my baby like that. We were going outside to get her off him. She was wrong for jumping on his ass, and I would have addressed that had he not manhandled her. My focus shifted quickly.

Anissa drove in silence until I said, "I'm sorry for you seeing what you saw. I just couldn't *not* protect and defend my baby."

She frowned as she glanced at me. "You have no reason to apologize, Sheldon. None. I feel you, baby. I really do. What did the police say?"

"We were let go without charges since we were at my house, but he can still file against us. I don't know if he will, since he wanted to be a hard nigga and sling my daughter like a rag doll. He had to know that I was there. That shit was bold. I was going out there to get her off him. She was wrong for attacking him, but the force he used to get her off him was unacceptable."

Anissa softly slid her hand over mine and offered me a sympathetic smile. Within minutes, we were in the hospital parking lot. I hopped out as soon as the car was in park, along with Shy. I'd forgotten his ass was even in the car. He was quiet as hell. I went to Anissa's door and helped her out, then we powerwalked to the ER.

The minute we walked in, I saw Chad and Isaiah. They rushed me, both asking questions at the same time. "Let's sit. Tell me how Alexz is doing first."

"She's in surgery," Chad said as Dylan came out of the restroom. When he saw Shy, Anissa, and me, he put some pep in his step. As if knowing what I would ask, he said, "Her arm is broken in two places. She said she heard and felt it crack when she landed. It's gonna take that shit a minute to heal. They brought that nigga to St. Elizabeth, since that was the closest hospital from your house."

"Good for him," Shyrón said.

I could still hear the aggression in his tone. He had a bruise on his face, and his hands were just as swollen as mine were. "How long did they say baby girl would be in surgery?"

"Well, they are thinking an hour or two, since the breaks weren't as bad as they originally thought. Alexz been drinking her milk."

I exhaled as DJ walked in and hugged his mother then slapped hands with my sons and loosely shook my hand. The main thing was that she would be okay. After knowing that, it seemed my adrenaline slowed down to damn near nothing, and I could feel exactly how much my hands were hurting. I was too damn old to be fighting, but that was better than me going back to the house to get my gun. Knowledge had better be glad I didn't do just that.

I'd be in jail, and my baby would have something totally different to worry about.

Anissa and I had just left church, and I felt good. I loved leaving church with my spirit feeling heightened. Alexz had gone home from the hospital yesterday. She refused to stay at my house because she said Anissa and I needed our time alone, so she went to Shy's place. He wouldn't have had it any other way. Anissa had catered to my and his needs after we'd left the hospital. Shy crashed at my house that night, and Anissa stayed with me too.

It was a little emotional having her stay at my house. The only woman to stay there was Marie. My counselor and I had spoken about that this past Thursday. I was going to ask her to stay with me anyway before all the drama happened. After lying next to her for two nights in New Orleans, I didn't want to let that feeling go.

I knew it was too soon to ask her to move in… at least too soon for her. I was ready, or so I thought I was. I hadn't even declared my love for her yet. I loved Anissa with my whole heart, but I knew if I expressed that so soon, it could give her pause. I didn't want her to feel like I was trying to pressure her into anything. I was just a fast mover when things felt right, whatever the case was, and I respected my gut.

My counseling session had gone so well, she suggested I make an appointment whenever I felt I needed another one. My mind was made up, and my heart was convinced that Anissa was the woman for me. That didn't make me love Marie any less. It was beyond time to move on, and subconsciously, my heart had been waiting on the day a woman would walk into my life and turn it upside down.

That was probably why it attached itself to Anissa so quickly. People said all the time that when you knew, you knew. I didn't think they meant this damn fast though. Maybe with as long as the both of us had suffered, we were drawn to one another's pain. Whatever the reason, I was happy that it happened just the way that it did, because once I gave in completely, my soul opened up in ways I'd forgotten it could.

When we got to my house, I was surprised to see everyone was already there. "Well, shut up and shoot me. I can't believe they're all here already."

Anissa chuckled as she parked in my driveway. She'd been driving me around since I'd hurt my hands. Although I felt fine now, she insisted on me resting my hands as much as possible. She babied me in a way that I'd never known. Marie wouldn't dare. After getting out and opening her door, she said, "Maybe they're hungry."

"Maybe so."

Anissa and I had cooked together before church, although it was mainly her cooking and me watching, since she had me on restriction. I didn't care that she wanted to take care of me, so long as she took care of me tonight. It had been a few days, and I was long overdue. My dick had gone into shock, wondering how I could provide him with that good shit only to deprive him of it now.

After walking into the house and speaking to everybody, Anissa and Isaiah began getting the food warmed. I went and sat next to my baby girl. "How you feeling today, baby?"

"I'm good, Daddy. Thank you for always having my back, even when I'm wrong. I know I shouldn't have hit him. I learned my lesson this time. I remember you used to always tell me that just because my brothers were brought up not to hit girls, that I shouldn't take advantage of that. One day I would meet a boy that wasn't taught that and have the whole family in jail. That could have been so much worse. I'm so sorry for getting you and Shyrón caught up in my bullshit."

"How many times do I have to tell you? I'm your dad. It's my job to have your back."

She laid her head on my arm, and I leaned over and kissed it. "Have you made a final decision about what you're going to do?"

She lifted her head, immediately knowing that I was speaking about her pregnancy. "Yeah. I have appointments Tuesday and Wednesday. You think Ms. Anissa would come with me?"

"Absolutely. But for some reason, if she can't, I wouldn't have a problem being there with you."

"I know."

She laid against me again then grabbed my hand and lightly rubbed it between hers until Isaiah and Anissa called us to the table. I had an eight-chair dining table, so there were just enough seats. Last weekend, we'd scattered between the table and the front room since Jamel had joined us. Looked like I was just gonna have to invest in a larger banquet-style table. If any of them finally found someone to love, there wouldn't be enough room.

Alexz went to the kitchen for a moment, so I remained standing until she returned. Once Alexz, Shy, and I were seated, everyone began bringing food to the table. "Anissa, you gon' have to be careful about this. I don't wanna get used to this catering you're doing."

Chad rolled his eyes. "You gon' make my pops a whole babified ass nigga. We can't have that, Ms. Anissa, because I'm gon' stay on him about it. I know he don't want those problems in his life."

She giggled as she set my prepared plate in front of me. "But I like catering to you. So it's okay if you like it too."

She kissed the side of my head as she went back to the kitchen. I nodded then grinned at Chad. "Don't hate because you ain't got a woman... a good woman at that."

"Oh, I ain't hating. My time coming. I been scoping out this fly one at the gym for the past week."

"When you gon' approach her?" Dylan asked with a frown.

"Sit down, nigga. Let me work how I work. I like to pay attention first and learn what I can by watching. I'll make a move soon."

I slowly shook my head at their banter. Once Anissa rejoined us, everyone quieted down so I could lead us in grace. We all grabbed hands. I rested my hand on Alexz's shoulder since her injured arm was next to me. "Lord, thank You for gathering us all together under one roof, safe and sound. This weekend has been tough, but You brought us through. Thank You for Anissa, DJ, and Jamel. You've expanded our family, and we are grateful. Please bless the food we are about to consume, and bless the hands that prepared it. In Your name, amen."

I kissed Anissa's hand before releasing it then immediately lowered my gaze to the food before me. Just as I was about to dive into the mac and cheese, Chad said, "You know y'all owe me, right?"

I frowned as I stared at him, waiting for him to fill me in to just what he thought I owed him. Anissa giggled. I supposed she figured out what he was talking about. He continued. "Had it not been for my friendship with DJ and me convincing you to have that barbeque, y'all wouldn't have met. So I'ma need to see some appreciation 'round here."

Anissa excused herself and went to the kitchen. When she came back, she had a plate of some nasty ass tripe. She set it in front of Chad, and his eyes brightened. He loved tripe. "Aww shit! This what I'm talking 'bout! Let me go on and start calling you Mama. I'll hurt my dad if he mess this up."

Everybody laughed, but that was significant to me. To know that he felt that deep of a connection with her did my heart good. Chad was a fool, but he didn't usually say shit like that unless he meant it. Alexz leaned over to me and said, "Mama Nissa said yes."

She smiled brightly at me, and I couldn't help but smile back and nod. Everyone was happy, and that was what I wanted for my family. They seemed to take to her as quickly as I had. I grabbed Anissa's hand and said, "You don't have to worry about a thing. I won't mess this up, because you're a dream come true."

"I'm not worried. It was a part of God's plan for us to meet, and in time, I know we are meant for more than this. What He has joined together, no man will put asunder."

I smiled then kissed her lips. She was saying just what I had been thinking. She was the one, and in time, I would make it official. First, by professing my love for God's masterpiece, then making her my wife. *Anissa Berotte, wife of Sheldon and mother of seven.* She was who we all needed, and Chad was right. I owed him big time.

The End

If you did not read the author's note at the beginning, please go back and do so before leaving a review. 😊

FROM THE AUTHOR...

This story was extremely fast paced. Sheldon grabbed my hand and took off running, despite his reservations. That night after the barbeque, brother was on the fast track, and I didn't know what to do to slow his ass down. Anissa wasn't any better. She followed his lead. LOL! I loved the two of them together, and I love the stories that will emerge from this one. As you can probably tell, Alexz's story will be first. She has the most pressing issue out of the seven of them. As of right now, Dylan will be next, unless something more pressing happens with someone else in Alexz's book.

I really hope you enjoyed this story. As always, I gave it my all. Whether you liked it or not, please take the time to leave a review on Amazon and/or Goodreads.

There's also an amazing playlist on Apple Music and Spotify for this book, under the same title that includes some great R&B and rap tracks to tickle your fancy.

Please keep up with me on Facebook, Instagram, and TikTok (@authormonicawalters), Twitter (@monlwalters), and Clubhouse (@monicawalters). You can also visit my Amazon author page at www.amazon.com/author/monica.walters to view my releases.

FROM THE AUTHOR...

Please subscribe to my webpage for updates and sneak peeks of upcoming releases! https://authormonicawalters.com.

For live discussions, giveaways, and inside information on upcoming releases, join my Facebook group, Monica's Romantic Sweet Spot at https://bit.ly/2P2lo6X.

OTHER TITLES BY MONICA WALTERS

Standalones

Love Like a Nightmare

Forbidden Fruit (An Erotic Novella)

Say He's the One

Only If You Let Me

On My Way to You (An Urban Romance)

Any and Everything for Love

Savage Heart (A KeyWalt Crossover Novel with Shawty You for Me by T. Key)

I'm In Love with a Savage (A KeyWalt Crossover Novel with Trade It All by T. Key)

Don't Tell Me No (An Erotic Novella)

To Say, I Love You: A Short Story Anthology with the Authors of BLP

Drive Me to Ecstasy

Whatever It Takes: An Erotic Novella

When You Touch Me

When's the Last Time?

Best You Ever Had

Deep As It Goes (A KeyWalt Crossover Novel with Perfect Timing by T. Key)

The Shorts: A BLP Anthology with the Authors of BLP (Made to Love You- Collab with Kay Shanee)

All I Need is You (A KeyWalt Crossover Novel with Divine Love by T. Key)

This Love Hit Different (A KeyWalt Crossover Novel with Something New by T. Key)

Until I Met You

Marry Me Twice

Last First Kiss

Nobody Else Gon' Get My Love (A KeyWalt Crossover Novel with Better Than Before by T. Key)

Love Long Overdue (A KeyWalt Crossover Novel with Distant Lover by T. Key)

Next Lifetime

Fall Knee-Deep In It

Unwrapping Your Love: The Gift

Who Can I Run To

You're Always on My Mind

Behind Closed Doors Series

Be Careful What You Wish For

You Just Might Get It

Show Me You Still Want It

Sweet Series

Bitter Sweet

Sweet and Sour

Sweeter Than Before

Sweet Revenge

Sweet Surrender

Sweet Temptation

Sweet Misery

Sweet Exhale

Never Enough (A Sweet Series Update)

Sweet Series: Next Generation

Can't Run From Love

Access Denied: Luxury Love

Still: Your Best

Sweet Series: Kai's Reemergence

Beautiful Mistake

Favorite Mistake

Motives and Betrayal Series

Ulterior Motives

Ultimate Betrayal

Ultimatum: #lovemeorleaveme, Part 1

Ultimatum: #lovemeorleaveme, Part 2

Written Between the Pages Series

The Devil Goes to Church Too

The Book of Noah (A KeyWalt Crossover Novel with The Flow of Jah's Heart by T. Key)

The Revelations of Ryan, Jr. (A KeyWalt Crossover Novel with All That Jazz by T. Key)

The Country Hood Love Stories

8 Seconds to Love

Breaking Barriers to Your Heart

Training My Heart to Love You

The Country Hood Love Stories: The Hendersons

Blindsided by Love

Ignite My Soul

Come and Get Me

In Way Too Deep

You Belong to Me

Found Love in a Rider

Damaged Intentions: The Soul of a Thug

Let Me Ride

Better the Second Time Around

I Wish I Could Be The One

I Wish I Could Be The One 2

Put That on Everything: A Henderson Family Novella

What's It Gonna Be?

Someone Like You

Printed in Great Britain
by Amazon